THE
SHADOW
BEHIND
THE
STARS

THE
SHADOW
BEHIND
THE
STARS

REBECCA HAHN

 ATHENEUM BOOKS FOR YOUNG READERS
New York   London   Toronto   Sydney   New Delhi

ATHENEUM BOOKS FOR YOUNG READERS
An imprint of Simon & Schuster Children's Publishing Division
1230 Avenue of the Americas, New York, New York 10020
For information about special discounts for bulk purchases, please contact Simon & Schuster Special Sales at 1-866-506-1949 or business@simonandschuster.com.
The Simon & Schuster Speakers Bureau can bring authors to your live event. For more information or to book an event, contact the Simon & Schuster Speakers Bureau at 1-866-248-3049 or visit our website at www.simonspeakers.com.
Book design by Debra Sfetsios-Conover and Irene Metaxatos
The text for this book is set in Weiss Std.
Manufactured in the United States of America
First Edition
10 9 8 7 6 5 4 3 2 1
Library of Congress Cataloging-in-Publication Data
Hahn, Rebecca.
The shadow behind the stars / Rebecca Hahn. — First edition.
pages cm
Summary: Chloe, Serena, and Xinot, the Fates, live on a secluded island spinning, measuring, and cutting the threads of human life but when Aglaia, a mortal, finds them Chloe must try to keep her sisters from getting attached to the girl and involved in her dark fate that could unravel the world.
ISBN 978-1-4814-3571-0 (hardcover)
ISBN 978-1-4814-3573-4 (eBook)
[1. Fate and fatalism—Fiction. 2. Goddesses, Greek—Fiction. 3. Mythology, Greek— Fiction. 4. Prophecies—Fiction. 5. Oracles—Fiction.] I. Title.
PZ7.H12563Sh 2015
[Fic]—dc23 2014026428

For my brothers

THE
SHADOW
BEHIND
THE
STARS

PART ONE

One

THIS IS A STORY ABOUT THE END OF THE WORLD.

It is a lesson for you, mortal, so listen well to my words. Shiver and become them. When you sleep, dream of them. When you blink, see us sisters spinning, measuring, *slicing* in the darkness behind your lids.

Know us. Fear us. Heed my warning, mortal: Stay far away from us.

My name is Chloe, and I am the youngest. Mine are the fingers that choose the wool, that shape the thread, that begin it. The sun smiles upon me. Men love me without knowing who I am. I have lived forever and will live forever more.

By the beginning of this story, I had seen everything. Nothing was new to me, not in birth or death or living. There should have been nothing left that could surprise me.

Here is the thing about this world we spin, though: It is full of surprises. Live a thousand years, and you will be surprised on the thousand and first. That is the beauty of it—the impossible riddles, the dark. It is also the danger—how quickly your life twists suddenly inside out.

Even for us it is this way, immortal as we are. We can still be startled by the beauty, and the danger can still take us unaware. Even when we think we are ready for it; even when we know better.

We should have known better that first afternoon, when the girl showed up on our doorstep. We should have realized the danger she brought when we saw the dark pain in her gaze. Maybe then we could have stopped it; maybe then the end of the world never would have come.

Or then again, maybe it wouldn't have made any difference at all. My sister might still have cast her spell; the fish might still have jumped out of the waves before the girl. I don't know when it's ever done us good to know what's coming, after all. Mostly, there isn't anything that any of us can do.

This girl was young, only just beyond childhood, but she had already lost her family, her friends, everyone she knew. The raiders had come and killed them all; she had watched as they screamed, as they fell, as they slid from the edge into darkness. She had lain quite still and pretended to be as dead, while the men took what they wanted from her village and smashed to bits everything else. The girl felt, there in the bloody dust of the road, that she was being smashed to bits as well.

When they had gone, nothing was left of the life she had

known, and nothing was left of this girl but an unthinking urge, an ancient instinct to pick herself up, to stumble out through her village, not looking, not smelling, not hearing. She walked for days, for weeks. She followed that invisible pull through fields, across streams, not caring where the road went or how rough was the ground. She only walked on, and crawled when she couldn't walk, and at last she was climbing the steep rock slope between our crashing waves, balancing one step after another until she had reached our round green island. And then she stood, feet raw, in our doorway, looking in at us.

Not many make it that far. I'm sure you'll already know that.

She told us what had happened. Her eyes were flashing with what she had seen; her voice was harsh. When she had finished, she demanded that we tell her what there was to live for now.

She was so insistent that we tried to answer her. I listened to the whir of my whalebone spindle. Serena ran her fingers along the girl's gold thread, feeling every bump and twist. Xinot clicked her scissors—*click, clack*—and sniffed at the empty space where that thread came to an end, staring blankly all the while with her swirling eyes.

We stopped our whirring and fingering and sniffing. We looked at the girl.

There is nothing we can tell you, we said. *We know what your life is made of and its length. We can guess at the emptiness beyond. But we are not allowed to tell you what is to come, and we have never been told how a life ought to be used.*

Xinot turned back at once to sharpening her scissors on a rough gray rock. I gazed silently at the girl: at her locks, as golden as her long, long thread; at her eyes, blue as a summer sea. She was beautiful, even after that desperate journey. I found myself wondering what she might have looked like before—when she was still happy, when her eyes had flashed with joy.

Serena, though, didn't turn from the girl or watch her silently. Serena could not bear to send her away like that, and she stood from her chair and went over to the girl. She wrapped her arms around her, and the girl almost collapsed into them, closing her eyes and letting out her breath. The lines in her face relaxed as they mustn't have in the last two weeks, since the raiders first were spotted riding toward her town.

We have some magic beyond the spindle, the thread, and the scissors. Serena laid a hand on the girl's head and said, *Forget it all. Go, and start again.* She pressed her lips against the girl's forehead, stood her upright, and turned her from our door. The girl walked away, as we knew she would, as she must.

I shook my own dark, silky hair over the front of my shoulders and turned back to my spinning. I wouldn't wish for the girl's golden locks. She may have been happy once, but looks like that only ever led to trouble. Consider her—family dead, no reason to live, and decades, by Serena's measure, to steep in her pain, to wake in the middle of the night gasping through her tears.

Serena stood in the doorway two moments more, and then she took up her place in the chair between us again, stretching the newest thread from my spindle over toward Xinot's blades. She started a song, a ballad men sing as they board ships to war. I added a descant harmony, and Xinot hummed a low, pulsing undertone.

We returned to our work, and I imagined the girl climbing back along the narrow pathway to the mainland, Serena's words turning her mind into a pleasant fuzzy mush.

I was sure that she wouldn't be coming back. You mortals never did. You came, you made your impossible demands, and then you left again. It had been this way for ages, longer than any bard could remember. With luck it always would be this way.

You would think, being who I am, that I would be wary of making statements like this, even only in my own head. It's a tricky thing, the power we shape and measure and cut.

Get too full of your own cleverness, too certain—you'll find yourself marrying your mother, cutting out the heart of your father, eating your children's fingers for breakfast.

Three minutes after I'd mused, so certainly, on how none of our visitors ever came back, the girl with the golden locks showed up in our doorway once again.

That was the first surprise of that day.

My spindle jerked and skittered away over the stones. Serena dropped her thread with a soft cry. And Xinot almost— *almost*—*sliced* a man's thread off seven years too short, and it hung there, the half-severed thing, flashing red and silver. Then she drew the scissors wide and held her fingernails just where Serena had handed the thread to her. The blades *snapped* together with a harsh ring; the man's thread fell to the floor, pooling into an orderly mound just below Xinot's feet.

Then, silence.

The girl was smiling serenely around at us all. She held up a fat, flapping fish by its tail. "I was climbing over the rocks," she said, "and this fellow leaped out of the waves, threw himself right down before me. And I thought, you ladies must be so busy, with all your—work." Something skipped across her face; Serena's spell, I'd guess, fighting against the girl's doubtful thoughts. Then her olive-smooth brow eased. "And since you've been so helpful to me . . ."

"What is it she thinks we've done?" I whispered, and sent the words tumbling over to Serena.

My sister shrugged, her empty hands still frozen where they'd held the thread. "Whatever the spell's set her up to believe," she sent back.

". . . I thought I could begin to repay you by bringing you a nice tasty fish and cooking it up for you." There went that face skip again, as the girl considered our one-room house. We haven't much in the way of furniture: just a stool for me, and a plain wooden chair for Serena, and an old stump for Xinot, from a tree that died so long ago it never had a name. We've a fire pit in the very center sometimes, and sometimes a grill sits over the coals, or a tripod with a cauldron hanging between its legs.

But just now there were no coals, and no fire, and no pit. The girl blinked around, her mouth gaping and closing like the mouth of the fish that was sliding from her hands.

Xinot narrowed her eyes at Serena. "Do something," she hissed.

Serena jerked her head at that and lowered her hands. She cleared her throat—a comforting, melodious sound.

"Thank you, dear," she said. The girl stopped gaping, grasped the fish again, and focused on Serena's face as though it was the only thing she remembered.

Possibly it was. Serena was now this girl's first real memory, after all.

Serena said, in that gentle murmur only she can manage, "My dear, will you please tell my sisters your name?"

"Your sisters?" She blinked around at us now. "These are your—sisters?"

Serena laughed, low and bubbly. "I call them that, despite the vast difference in age. They are my closest living relations, all I have left in the world. *Your name, dear.*"

Not many would be capable of defying Serena when she's become insistent, and this girl was no exception. "Aglaia," she said at once, with a slight bow. "I am Aglaia."

"Lovely!" Serena clapped her hands and smiled at the girl. I had seen that expression on her face before, that warm softness as she talked with one of you. "It is a pleasure to meet you, Aglaia, and we will happily accept your gift."

"*Oh.*" Now the girl's face was shining. "Will you?"

"Yes, of course, if you will share it with us."

"Serena," I muttered, reminding her, "we've no business eating a meal with a mortal."

She eyed me and muttered back, "It's only one fish. It's nothing, Chloe." Then she turned to the girl again, laying a hand on my arm. "My youngest sister will show you where you can get the beast ready for cooking, down by our shore."

The girl tilted her head at me, so open, so trusting. Her eyes really were the color of our sunlit sea.

"Xinot," I started, turning toward my eldest sister. "Do you really think—"

She cut me off with a wave of her blades. "Oh, go on, Chloe," she said. "She won't bite you."

"Won't she?" But my sisters were looking at me expectantly, and I couldn't win against them both. "Fine," I said, sighing. "If you want to eat this fish so much, I suppose you'll need her out of the house while you start the fire."

"Exactly," Serena said.

So I slid my spindle into my basket with the wool. Then I grabbed Aglaia's arm, and I pulled the mortal girl from our house.

At the water's edge, we crouched down together, and Aglaia began to wash the fish. My toes curled along the side of a flat rock, my tunic pulled low over my ankles. My hair was whipping around my head; it does that sometimes, especially when I am wary of something or feeling some strong emotion. I watched as she scraped the scales with a sharp piece of shale and then used the stone to slice open the fish's belly. She did not speak; she wasn't paying me any mind. I bent over toward her, looking into her face. Her eyes went sideways, noting I was there, but she only turned up her lips at me and continued easing out the guts. I sat back again.

It isn't fair, the sort of life you mortals lead. Even forgetting death, even forgetting how little time you have to understand anything, there is so much difficulty that I sometimes wonder how you can keep on going. What had happened to Aglaia happens to someone every day. Mothers watch their children starve. Fathers are enslaved.

It is a marvel sometimes that you don't sit right down and give up. It is a marvel you don't scream at the gods for creating the world this way, that you can lift your head still, and smile, and want to live—that you can demand from us a reason to want to live.

I watched this girl; her hair was gleaming in the last of the sun's rays. No doubt he was delighted to have such a fresh little beauty to smile upon. "Your hair," I said at last, wondering at how it could still shine like that after all she'd gone through. "Your hair is quite beautiful."

Aglaia said, "Thank you," pronouncing each word clearly, with a small space between. Abruptly she turned toward me and reached out a slimy fish hand, as if wanting to show that she held no dangerous thing. "I am Aglaia."

"Yes," I said, leaning back, my hair spinning across my nose. "I know."

But she kept her hand held out, and she had a funny plastered-on smile that hadn't flickered or melted when I'd pulled away from her. So I slipped a hand from where I'd tucked it in my tunic and gripped hers, quickly. Then I slid it away again. "I'm Chloe."

"It is nice to meet you," said Aglaia.

I nodded, warily.

She turned back to her cleaning and didn't look at me again.

I waited as she finished, as she pulled the kidney from the fish and made to throw it and the guts into the sea.

"Don't!" I said, coming to my feet and reaching for her hand. We didn't need our shoreline smelling of fish guts, or our toes to squish in them when we visited the waves.

Aglaia stopped and stared at me, her mouth slightly open. She was blinking fast, as if recalculating her world.

I spoke slow, and low. "We have a garden. Let's bring the nasty stuff there and give it to the plants."

She looked down into her hand, where the guts were beginning to drip between her fingers. "Nasty stuff," she said.

"Come along." I gestured to her, and she followed me up the rocks, onto the green cap of our island. We went around to the back of the house, where Serena keeps our garden growing in the lee of our walls, out of the wind.

It's an impossible task, much of the time. The air is so salty, most things choke to death. Come one big storm in the growing season, and our whole crop fails. It's lucky we don't suffer from lack of food, or we'd never survive out here on our rock. Or we'd survive, but we'd be miserable every second, like that idealistic fellow who broke the rules and spent several eternities chained to a stone, watching birds eat out his liver every afternoon for lunch.

This year we'd had good fortune with the weather. Several small cabbages were growing in the shade of the house, and we'd have a large crop of onions and cucumbers. There were even some lentil pods almost ready for picking. I brought Aglaia over to our grapevines down the slope a bit. There was a doomed endeavor if I ever saw one. Our vines only ever grew tiny bitter fruit, hardly worth eating and certainly not of a quality for making wine. But Serena couldn't help trying. When we had lived on the mainland, many centuries ago, our vines had been the envy of every mortal and several gods as well. Our wine could make the dullest man dance; it could put the saddest old woman to sleep and give her wondrous dreams.

We missed our wine.

Aglaia and I spread the fish guts at the base of the vines, and I whispered to them, a gift-giving rhyme from a lovely altruistic culture that had lived nearby but had died out generations ago.

Then we went back down to the shore and we washed our hands with the help of the sea. I watched as Aglaia lifted the readied fish and started up the path to our house. She had done everything I had asked, simply and without argument. She had been so at ease, sitting by the water with me, and now each step she took was precise and unhurried. I remembered the harsh strength that had been in her voice this afternoon. She had seemed half-wild then, with her raw feet and flashing eyes—a wounded eagle, not a nesting wren.

I called after her, curious, "Aglaia, where do you think we are?"

She stopped and looked back at me, a line between her eyes. "Don't you know?"

I shook my head at her.

The line deepened. "I think . . ." She looked about at the waves, at the rocks, at the orange light we could see now flickering through our door at the top of the hill. "I think I've come to stay with you. I think this is home." Her face was smoothing out. "Yes, Chloe. This is where I live. This is our home." She smiled. It was a big, sparkling smile, the sort that mothers stitch onto their daughters' dolls. She said, with a bit of a laugh, "Come on! They're waiting for us." And she took off up the slope again, grasping the fish tight in her hands.

I stood there staring after her. She didn't yet know my sisters' names. And . . . *home?* I wasn't sure even I considered this our home. Home was for babies and growing old. This was a place to live, a place to do our work.

But Aglaia was far ahead now, and the others were shortly in for a second surprise. I couldn't imagine how Xinot was going to react to an addle-brained mortal girl calling this her home. She would have to agree with me now; she would have to throw Aglaia out as soon as she heard. She might even apologize for not arguing with Serena about the meal. I sucked in a breath and started eagerly up the slope after the girl. It wasn't often that my sister admitted she was wrong. I wasn't going to miss this for all the stars and their songs.

Two

WHILE AGLAIA AND I HAD BEEN OUT WASHING
the fish, my sisters had gotten a fire blazing in our pit. Xinot
sat on her stump near the edge, poking at the cinders with
her cane. The dark wood took no harm from the heat; it
wasn't an ordinary sort of thing, with ordinary obedience to
physical laws. She didn't look up as Aglaia and I came over
with the girl's gift, but she tapped the metal grill she'd set
upon the coals so that it clanged a bit, and the girl placed
the fish on it.

Then Aglaia drew my stool over next to her and sat down,
resting her elbows on her knees. My sisters eyed me, Serena
with worry and Xinot with a gleam of amusement.

I shrugged and settled onto the stones on the other side of
the fire. I could view my vindication just as happily from here.

I was in for a wait, though. Serena came over and placed

her usual chair next to me, and we were all silent for a bit, watching the fish cook. It was the perfect time for them to question our uninvited guest. There she was, sitting in *my* place, bending over our fire as if she belonged. And my sisters hardly glanced at her. Xinot kept poking at the fire with her stick. Serena was sewing some useless thing—you'd think, after working with the thread all day, she would be sick of all forms of needlework, but Serena's always knitting us caps and tacking together bits of yarn and cloth to hang on the wall. All pointless, as Xinot and I would never hide our hair from the wind, and there's hardly room on our walls for anything but shelves and piles of thread. Still, she keeps at it. She spins her own yarn out of the little grasses that grow along our rocks. I think she must use her magic for it, as it seems an impossible task.

She was busy with something—a cushion for her chair, I think; her old one was beginning to fray—and she didn't seem the slightest bit concerned with the girl she'd just bespelled. She pulled at her yarn and hummed to herself, mulling over some secret thing.

I glared across the fire at Aglaia. She smiled back at me. I glared harder; she smiled more. So I scowled into the fire instead and joined my sisters in ignoring her completely. One more hour; one shared meal. If the girl hadn't declared her intention by then, I would give up the satisfaction of seeing my sisters uncover it themselves, and I would give fate a hand.

When the fish was done, we apportioned it into four drift-wood bowls, though we are never in danger of starving and could have saved the whole creature for the girl. Xinot ate silently; Serena made approving noises. I picked at mine at first, but the smell was too exquisite, and soon I was tucking into it as eagerly as the others. We're never in danger of starving, but a fresh grilled fish is as tasty in our mouths as yours.

Then we threw the bones to the fire, though I saw the way Xinot flicked her fingers toward them, and I knew she would have liked to toss them over the stones to uncover some fortunes. Not the most accurate of fortune-telling tools, fish bones, but when they aren't spewing nonsense they are dramatic. Filled to every curve and ridge with stories of hidden jewels and questing princes.

This girl was already getting in the way of even our smallest pleasures. I had done enough waiting. "Aglaia," I said, and she smiled at me. "What did you say this place was again? My sisters would like to know."

Serena looked up from her work, frowning from me to the girl. She had coaxed Aglaia into draping her cloak near the fire while I served the fish. It had warmed as we ate, and now my sister was busy patching its tears and fraying edges.

"I told you," said Aglaia, "this is home."

The silence following that statement was all that I had wished for.

"What did you say?" said Xinot, twisting on her stump to stare at the girl.

Aglaia said again, as matter-of-factly, "This is home."

"Your home?" said Xinot.

"Ours," said Aglaia.

Xinot opened and then closed her mouth, for once at a loss. I raised my eyebrows at Serena, who was furrowing her brow at me as though I held the answer to this, as though this was some trick I had worked up when I was out with the girl.

I muttered, "It's *your* spell."

"I didn't mean . . ." Serena tucked her needle into her skirt and cleared her throat, leaning over toward the girl.

She said softly, "Aglaia, dear, I'm afraid you can't stay here."

"Why not?"

"Well . . ." Serena looked to me again; I shook my head.

"You know she doesn't remember," I said.

Aglaia said, "Why can't I stay here? Where am I to go?" She was still perfectly placid, but there was confusion in her voice, and maybe a note of desperation. The world would seem so simple to her now, and we were denying what she knew of the shape of it.

Xinot said, finally, nodding at the girl, "She's right."

"What do you mean?" said Serena. "That this is her home?" "Don't be ridiculous."

I let them come to the obvious solution; I watched the girl as they spoke. She seemed to already have forgotten that we were discussing her. She was leaning back on my stool, gazing into the fire. I thought I heard the beginning of a humming tune drifting across the pit.

"Then what are you saying?" said Serena.

Xinot said, "We can't throw her out, not with whatever your spell did to her. Her mind is lost; look at her."

My sisters turned as well toward Aglaia, who continued to

sit and lean and hum. The firelight brushed the ends of her hair, and the humming floated, soft and strange. She seemed a thing apart, untethered.

Xinot said, in her hard, low way, "I know you didn't mean for this to happen. But now you have to take the spell away."

Serena didn't respond; she kept on watching the girl, and I saw a shiver dance across her skin.

"Even if we could keep her, sister, this is no home for her. You've seen her thread, how bright it is. Do you think she should burn for all those years out here with us? With our bare rocks and empty wind?"

Serena said, "She's happier this way. There is no home for her out there, either."

Then they were silent, remembering what Aglaia had fled.

When Xinot spoke again, it was more quietly, and she sat back on her stump so that her eyes seemed even darker, even deeper-set than usual. "This isn't a cat."

"A cat?" Aglaia looked up at this, eager. "Do we have a cat?"

Serena reached out to brush the girl's cheek, so terribly tender. "Not anymore."

I was shuddering. Xinot would have to put a stop to this. She would have to snatch our sister's fingers away from the girl's smooth skin, to toss Aglaia out our door, spell or no spell. If Serena wouldn't give her back her mind, she would have to do without it, and without us.

Aglaia said, her eyes on Serena's face, "Is that my cloak you are sewing?"

"Yes, child."

"Oh," said Aglaia, a breath. "How good you are to me."

We couldn't *keep* her. We couldn't let Serena look at her that way, with kindness. It would kill her. It would end up killing us. I turned to Xinot, and I saw her eyes sliding my way. I didn't have to speak; she knew my thoughts. We almost always do. But my eldest sister sat silent, leaning back on her stump. Something had sent her into her old manner of watching, waiting, an enigma in the dark. She shrugged at me with her bony shoulders, as if to say there was nothing to be done.

I wanted to scream at them. I wanted to grab this mortal girl and throw her out myself.

But the weight of one sister's choice and the silence of the other held me still. I have never been the first of us three. Serena speaks most; Xinot knows most. I am the quickest, the loveliest, the readiest to anger. I do not decide such things as whether an orphaned girl should be given a bed in our house.

Serena picked up her sewing again, and Xinot sat back and said nothing. I rose, frustrated, from the stones and went to sit against a far wall, shaking my hair closed about my face and glowering at nobody.

The girl I was sure would be our doom hummed to herself for a while longer. Then she got to her feet as well and wandered over to the nearest shelf, reaching out a curious hand toward our glittering towers of threads.

Apparently Xinot did think there was something she could do about *this*; she was up and next to the girl faster than I could blink. She grabbed Aglaia's raised arm with tight, crooked fingers. The girl turned, startled, and her mouth made a little O.

Before Serena's spell took it away, I saw the naked fear there, the horror in her eyes.

That was the third surprise, and the most unsettling—the strength of that horror, the way it had outlasted Serena's spell.

Then Aglaia's eyes went dim again; she relaxed her arm in Xinot's hold. My sister took her by her shoulders, lightly, and turned her from the shelves.

I felt a tension in my wrists. When I looked down, my fists were clenched and trembling.

"Come sit next to me, dear," Serena said. Her head was bent; she was still stitching away at the cloak. She looked up at me as Aglaia obediently moved across the room toward her. She smiled, and it was so unruffled, so clear and calm, I knew she hadn't seen the thing on Aglaia's face.

I whispered a word to my hands, and they unclenched. Before Serena could read something in my frown, I managed to send a small smile her way. I don't think it was very convincing, but she brightened anyway. That's all it takes with Serena, usually. A smile, a hug. She lives for our happiness, Xinot's and mine.

As Aglaia knelt down on the stones next to Serena, putting her head on my sister's knee and beginning to hum again, Xinot turned back to the shelf and nudged and shifted the coiled threads into perfect order. There was no need. Aglaia hadn't actually touched them. But Xinot stood there for several minutes, poking and twisting and tucking in glowing strands. When she turned away finally, I caught her eye before she ducked her head.

She knew. Xinot had seen the fear too, and the strength of it bothered her.

Maybe we could have told Serena, hoping to convince her to let the girl go. If our sister had realized the extent of the horror her spell was keeping buried, she might not have thought it a good idea to repress such a powerful thing. But even I didn't want to expose our sister to that pain. Not Serena, for whom a smile, a hug was the bright sun shining on her. Not Serena, who had only recently begun to smile again herself.

And anyway, Xinot and I didn't fully understand it either. We never have, that sort of human nightmare. We've never understood the depth of it, the way it lasts and lasts. For us, everything is temporary. Oceans change their currents. Borders shift and blur; even mountains fall. Soon enough, everything returns to the way it was before.

For you mortals, forever is a much more manageable term. One lifetime—that's all forever takes. One death, and forever is achieved. For you, horror and pain and grief really can last forever.

Serena kept on with her sewing. I retreated behind my hair. Xinot watched the girl from the corners of her eyes, and our fire crackled.

Late that night we went out to stand by the sea as we always did, and we left the girl curled up on a pile of Serena's knit blankets against one wall. She had tucked herself in cozily, calling out good night to us as if she had known us all her life.

Serena called back to her; Xinot and I said nothing. We left for the waves as soon as we knew she was asleep.

As we stood there, salt on our lips and moonlight tangling our hair, I didn't speak to the others about Aglaia. I wanted to forget her; I wanted to pretend there was nothing on our island but my sisters and the words brought by the wind. I closed my eyes; I breathed; and it should have been easy there.

After all, we are the daughters of the night. Xinot is the eldest, and I am young as a girl, but we all awoke at the same dark moment in the beginning of everything. When we go out to the edge of our rock and watch the stars spin, we remember where we came from, and we become more of who we are.

We need sleep even less than we need to eat. We could keep working with our threads all through the night if we wanted, but that's not what keeps us awake. There is always work to do, and the more we work, the more there seems to be. So we don't worry about that. Long ago, we used to fret much more. When even the sun was young, we wore our fingers to the bone trying to keep up with the piles of shining wool that never diminished in my basket. We thought that if we stopped, the wool would overflow, and mortals would not be born or live or die, and we would have destroyed the world.

But my heap of work never grows or shrinks. It is always exactly the same, whether we work on it or not. We've never stopped altogether. We take breaks. We garden. We never leave our work for more than several hours at a time.

Still, we do not worry about spending time away from the

threads, and we do not work at night unless our fingers are itching for it.

Instead we go out to the moon and the waves and the wind. We stand or sit along our shore, not next to one another, but we know where the others are.

We don't do anything in particular, not that you would recognize as action. We watch it, the way the world breathes in the night. Sisters of darkness—it is one name for us, and an apt one. Things are hidden in the dark. Things are unknown and inescapable. We might not always understand our own art, but we can feel it. We can taste it in the air on a clear, cold night. We can smell it in the brine when a storm is brewing over the waters. We are only sitting or standing, and listening to the prayers of the day, but we are also at some deeper level conversing with the magic that fills our threads.

When we watch and listen in this way, we become a thing that has meaning, that takes joy in each breath. Every night, we fill ourselves up with this joy, and then we spin and measure ourselves out and we provide the perfect endings each day.

That night, as Aglaia lay sleeping in the house at our backs, our magic was swirling and flowing in a strangely deliberate way. When I closed my eyes to forget the girl, I could almost hear it speaking. A soft murmur drifted all about, rising and falling, as though telling some great story—the sort that cannot be stopped once it has begun, the sort that holds you captive until the end.

It seemed . . . directional. And yes, when I concentrated, I could sense it sweeping over and around us, across our island, toward the house and our sleeping guest. It was gathering there, the magic, the stuff of our infinite work. It was interested in her; it had some claim to her.

I opened my eyes and looked over at my sisters. Serena was smiling up into the moon, which was full that night. Mine is the waxing moon, and Xinot's is the waning, but our middle sister loves the bright shining moon, all round and brilliant.

Xinot, though, was frowning. She had felt the flow of our dark magic too, and she didn't like it any more than I did. It seemed Aglaia wasn't just a poor lost thing after all; it seemed it would be harder to forget her than I had hoped. She had a future; we knew that from her thread. And our darkness seemed to be saying that hers was a stronger, deeper destiny than we had guessed.

Xinot turned her shadowed face toward mine. I knew her thoughts. We could tell Serena; we could ask her again to take the spell from Aglaia and send her off to meet this fate, mind and painful memories returned. We could set her free, and free ourselves of her.

But Xinot shook her head, and looked away again. I bunched my fists into my tunic, turning my face to the wind as well. Fine, then. I would have to find some other solution to this. As much as I did not like to admit it, Xinot was right. It was too risky—even if we told Serena how powerful this girl's fate was, we couldn't be sure our sister would allow Aglaia to leave. She might want to help; she might take the girl further into her arms. What was cloak-mending today might become cooking lessons tomorrow, or giving her the names of toads, or telling her ancient tales. Serena loved the brightly shining ones, and Aglaia's thread was as brilliant as tonight's moon.

So we let it go; again we stayed silent. We touched the drifting darkness and we listened to the waves. Aglaia slept. Serena watched the moon.

I shivered, and I hoped the foreboding I felt was only our magic whispering nonsense, some warped game. I hoped, but I could not believe it was that toothless. Since we opened our eyes in the midst of that first eternal night, it has been ours— the darkness, the threads, the sweet beginnings and bitter ends, the whole messy tangle of mortal life. In some ways, there is little difference between us sisters and our art: When I am working my spindle, I am the masses of glittering wool, and the whirring tool, and the edges of my fingers as they coax each fresh thread into existence. Serena is the length, the priceless single strand that slides along her palm, one long golden afternoon. Xinot is a thousand, a million, countless *snaps*, only just touching the thread, inevitable nothings.

We are one another, the hands that pass the thread, connecting us to the others, beginning to middle to end.

So we know more than anything how it twists and turns, how one wrong tug undoes it all. There was danger on the wind tonight; there was danger in this wandering girl. It was so close, and I knew just how easily we could fall into it. If Serena would not take her spell away, if Xinot would not turn Aglaia out, then I would have to do something myself to get rid of her, and soon.

Three

THE MORNING AFTER AGLAIA ARRIVED, AS SOON as she had awoken, I took her out to sea in our boat.

It was only a little wooden skiff, and my sisters and I hardly used it. Mostly, we never left our island, not to go out to sea, not to visit the mainland. There was enough right where we were to occupy us. The wind would blow until we tasted salt with every breath. Or the sea would calm so still, you'd think you could step across it as across a clear glass floor.

If you've never lived by the sea, you might not understand the way the world shifts so thoroughly at its edge. We didn't leave our rock, but it transformed from day to day, as did the colors of the waves and the texture of the sky. We stayed, unaltered; even our clothes never tore or grew so soiled one dip in the sea couldn't freshen them. But all about us, gulls twisted, and rocks crumbled off and were swept back to shore, and the whole earth melted and billowed itself into an endless variety of forms.

It reminded us of the limitations of our powers. That was another reason we went outside every night: to feel the galaxies sweeping over us, and to remember anew how very small we were, how unable to alter the threads that wove through each of our days, and how useless—how blasphemous—it would be to wish it otherwise.

We had not always been so isolated. Once, long ago, we had lived among you mortals on the mainland, and we had seen you almost every day. Some of you traveled great distances just to sample our wine. Others thought we would answer questions or even spin new fortunes. We wouldn't, of course, and we soon turned these away, but it didn't keep you from coming. It was too tempting, I suppose—the idea that there might be a shortcut past the harder parts of life.

We hadn't returned your visits; we were solitary, even then. I liked the awe of mortals, the way you cast down your eyes and stood aside to let me pass. Especially the young, muscled men, the ones with calloused hands and life pouring through them. I did not speak to them, but I liked to think that they would have done my bidding, had I asked it. And Xinot didn't engage with you even as much as I did. She slipped by you as a drifting chill. She sat silent on her stump when visitors came, and she stared off into nothing, and the shadows gathered around her.

The human children, though, had been somehow drawn to my middle sister, and she to them. Serena used to play with them out in their fields—games of chase, dancing rhymes, and braiding hair and flowers. She had favorites, first one child, and then another as that one grew. She spent more time with these, teaching them crafts and the language of trees, bringing them home to feed them sometimes. She loved to watch them grow.

At first, when her children passed into adulthood, and then old age, and finally left her completely, Serena had only smiled sadly and let them go. There were always more children, after all—some of them the daughters and sons of earlier ones. But Serena had always felt herself too much a mother. And mothers aren't meant to watch their children grow old, and older, and then disappear. They aren't meant to go on living after their children have gone.

It ate away at her. Not all at once, but we could see the sadness growing in her eyes. Xinot had worried more than I did. I thought Serena would stop caring so much, once she realized there was nothing to be done. Xinot, though, began to suggest that our sister stop taking in new children, that she give up this game. Every morning she would beg Serena to stay home, not to go out to the fields where the little ones ran after butterflies and one another. Every morning Serena would say, "I'll stay tomorrow. Just give me this one more day, and then I will be content."

And tomorrow she would say the same, and tomorrow and tomorrow. And the sadness leaked from her eyes and spread across her face, and she didn't smile anymore.

She began to sigh as she measured the thread. Her fingers

moved as flawlessly, and she passed the thread as smoothly. But she didn't join in when we sang our tunes, and she held herself so poised, so tense on her chair that I half expected her to turn to stone, and shatter.

It added a dangerous glint to our art. As the days went on, it became more and more difficult to time our movements, to create a rhythm and flow. There was a thinness to our work, an on-edgeness that made it seem as though our lengths and our *snap*s were limited, as though we would soon be wringing the very air for our bits of fluff.

I stayed away from my sisters, those last weeks on the mainland. I spent my free hours out walking through our vineyards, ripping one leaf after another from the vines. I'd snarl at them, and they'd burst into flames. For days, all I saw when I closed my eyes were those drifting bits of ash.

Xinot's usual irritation also grew as our sister melted into herself. When you mortals dropped by, she'd snap before you'd crossed the threshold, demanding to know what you wanted, glaring with utter malice. You backed away, more times than not, and left without saying a word.

She was ever gentle with Serena, though. I could hardly bear to look at our grieving sister, but I saw Xinot holding her hand, humming a soft, sweet tune—our Xinot, being kind. And when Serena wasn't doing anything but sitting in her chair and staring into the fire, when she had even given up all her sewing projects, her long, fair hands folded listlessly in her lap, it was Xinot who made the decision to leave.

Serena wasn't capable of protest. And I wanted nothing

more to do with mortals. I wanted my sister back; I wanted our work to be simple and full of joy. We agreed one evening that we would go, and we were gone with our wool and threads by morning. We told no one; only Serena's pack of children would have missed us, and we didn't want to see them. Not then, not ever again. We went far out, to the edge of land and beyond; we disappeared from mortal life. It was so pure on our island. There were no children, no visitors, no distractions. Once in a generation a hero made his way to our door, asked a question, and went away again. The rest of the time it was only us, and our threads, and all their glory.

See, the danger in you mortals is that you are so often at odds with your fate. You rail against it; you suffer because of it; you die. Yet in order to work our magic, we must believe in it. We must love the beauty of our threads, shiver at the mystery that lies at either end, catch our breaths at the wonder of our shaping. When we do, the thread runs smooth and the spindle whirs soft and the scissors *snap* clean and fast. When we believe in our work—when it is smooth and soft, clean and fast—we brush up against a power deeper than you could imagine. It is a power deeper than gods, deeper even than us three sisters. It forms our work; it gives our makings breath. It's a hidden pattern, a silent promise, the shadow behind the stars.

We can control this power, in a way. We can use it to form a minor fortune-telling, as Xinot does with her fish bones. We can fill ourselves with it, so that any of you mortals looking us in the face would feel a great awe rushing through you, like a wind. We can speak words, and they will echo with terrible truths, and it will be we who have chosen to let them free.

The power that we thus use, though, is not merely a slave to our will. It is much more dangerous than that. It is a thing as old as mortals; the gods do not know where it came from. It is a power so great, it is invisible, and it is weightless. It is gravity; it is direction.

We must believe in its rightness. We must believe so thoroughly that when we touch this power, we become it—the spinning and the drawing out and the *slicing*. If we don't believe, we sing off-key, we struggle with the thread. And we cannot afford to struggle; we cannot risk mistakes, because mistakes that creatures such as us make are more than deadly. They can be cataclysmic. They can be world ending.

That first morning, as Aglaia and I dragged the skiff from its usual home between two large rocks, we left Xinot muttering riddles and Serena sewing hats in our house. I had told my sisters we were going out to fish, and they had nodded, looking relieved. Aglaia would need much more food than we did, and my sisters had never taken to fishing.

I took the lines and the hooks with us, and I dug in our garden for some grubs. Aglaia slipped the slimy things into a pouch at her waist, without a complaint, not even wrinkling her nose at them. So we were all prepared for a fishing trip, but I had lied to my sisters. I didn't mean to feed the girl. I meant to drown her.

My sisters would be angry, I supposed—even Xinot would not approve of blatant murder. But I had to do something. Never mind that Aglaia's thread was so long it towered above the others on its shelf, never mind how the darkness had gathered around her last night. I thought of Xinot, who would not let her face show as she tidied the threads, for fear that we would see the horror reflected there; I thought of Serena, who was already much too involved with this orphaned girl. I was determined to take Aglaia's destiny into my own hands, to keep my sisters and our work safe.

Along with the fishing gear, I added a sturdy rope to the bottom of our skiff before we pushed off the island. Aglaia saw me shove it under my seat, but she didn't say a word. In fact, all the while I rowed us out into the sea, she sat across from me, looking at me amiably. There were no shadows in her eyes.

When we were far enough out that there was only water and sky in any direction, I took the rope from beneath my seat. I considered the girl.

It would be the simplest thing in the world, to bind Aglaia's hands, to tilt her into the waves. She wouldn't even know it was happening; Serena's spell would ease her suffocation, and she would swallow water easily and go without any struggle.

Well, it was possible that the magic would slip away from her at the end. As her mind darkened and her heartbeat slowed, she might open her eyes, aware at last of the tightening hold of the water. She might panic, white bursts of shock shooting through her brain. She might suffer after all.

But then never again.

Even in her half-aware state, this girl was beautiful. It may have been that beauty that made me hesitate before I killed her—the way the sun was playing at the ends of her hair, the way her eyes reflected the shifting sea. For a moment, as I watched her, I saw the world in this girl. But I think it was more than that. If I hadn't seen the moment by the threads when the dark fear had crossed her face, or if I hadn't felt our magic swirling around her—I would have wondered, maybe, but I would have let her go.

Those beginnings had shown how dangerous this girl might be. But I work the same thread as my sisters, and the hints at deepness also tantalized me.

Before I drowned her, I laid my fingers along Aglaia's cheekbone. I murmured a rhyme that undoes snarled things—I hadn't one strong enough to take away Serena's spell completely, but I could grant this girl a momentary clarity.

I saw her blink; I saw the shudder go all through her skin. I pulled away from her, back to my own seat, behind my hair.

She was breathing heavily. Her hands were gripping her bench, and I felt my heart beating fast as I watched her lift her head and open her eyes.

The horror that had flashed last night was back; it rattled her breath and shook her frame. She looked about, at the sky, down into the boat, and up to me. I don't think she was seeing any of it. I don't think she was wondering what she was doing out in the middle of the ocean—my untangling spell didn't allow for uncertainty.

When she caught my gaze again, I knew she was going to speak, and suddenly I didn't want to know what she would say. Oh, she was so beautiful—a thousand times more radiant than she was under Serena's spell. She was in pain, but full of purpose, and full of rage. I knew that as she opened her mouth—I knew the tone of her voice before she said it: "They weren't raiders, Chloe. Those bastards knew the secret way in under the village wall."

The anger I had anticipated, but I was frozen under the sure, cold knowledge in her words. She was telling me something important; it was a secret that she hadn't known when she showed up on our doorstep only yesterday. She was glaring at me. She was expecting me to speak. I faltered—I, the steadiest of my sisters!—and did what the mortal wanted. I said, "Are you certain?"

"They knew," she said. She leaned toward me, and that bright day was glinting like blue fire in her eyes. "They never opened the gate; they were there before we realized it. And—and they knew *me*. They pointed; they recognized me."

She was only a girl, some orphaned child Serena had felt sorry for. I had spun her thread. I had spun a thousand threads as tragic as this girl's.

But I was shivering. I pulled farther away from her.

"Chloe—" she started to say, and I saw her blink, hard. I thought she might be crying; I turned my face so I would not see her tears. "Chloe—" she said again; it was desperate. I looked, and she was staring, all still, as though gripped in some tight hold. Her lips fluttered once, wordless.

And then, between one blink and the next, her breath went out, and her face calmed.

Her shoulders relaxed; when she looked at me again, her eyes were dim. She blinked again, but slowly, and she leaned back on her seat, looking lazily across the waves.

I stared at her, still quivering. The sea was so silent, and the sun warmed us so pleasantly. My hair whipped much too frantically for such a calm scene, such a lovely girl sitting peaceably across from me.

The sun asked me what was wrong, but I didn't answer him. I supposed Aglaia had been as self-aware, as *alive* when she first showed up at our door. But then she had been like any of the wandering heroes we've had come to our island, scattered over the eons: temporary, disconnected from us. Sharing a boat in the middle of the sea, telling me her secrets, she had become someone individual; I knew her now.

I couldn't kill her. I wanted to, still. Oh, how I wanted to let her sink out of my sight, to forget her voice and the fiery way she had looked at me. I wanted never to think about this girl again.

Turning my face to the depths of the sea, I cursed the wonder that had made me take the spell away. Why had I needed to know? She was only another mortal, another poor creature caught up in our web. I knew what happened to such creatures. There was only ever one end.

I shoved the rope back under my seat, and I took out the fishing lines. Aglaia smiled sweetly as I showed her how to bait a hook, and I scowled and wished her safely drowned. But after the sea had granted us three fat fish, and they were slapping against our hull, mouths gaping as this girl's did, watching them, I brought her back to our island, and I helped her from the boat.

That afternoon my sisters and I sat in our usual places and worked. Aglaia waded out along our shore, watching minnows dart and gathering smooth, bright stones. She was piling a small collection in a corner by the blankets where she had slept last night. They were gleaming, empty things—not a speckle or a rough spot in the bunch.

As the sun dipped low, Aglaia put a fish over the fire to grill. She sat on the floor by the pit, watching our latest thread shimmering in the late summer light, passing from spindle to palm to *slice*. She rubbed her new collection in her hands, all over, around and about again. Each of her movements was spare, and exact, and as smooth as the stones.

I didn't tell my sisters what Aglaia had said in the boat, not as we worked and not as we stopped to eat the fish by our fire. After we ate, Serena picked up her hats again. She showed the stitches now and then to Aglaia, who put down her stones to finger the stuff, blinking wide.

Xinot was watching me over the top of her cane. I was sitting a bit away from them, tucking my knees up and folding my face in behind my hair. I could sense my sister's bottomless eyes, her knowing mouth.

"What bothers you, Chloe?" she murmured. The others were laughing at something; or Serena was laughing and Aglaia was joining in.

I didn't answer; I hunched lower.

Xinot curled her fingers, inviting. "You can tell me."

"Nothing," I muttered. "Leave me alone."

She sniffed, but she turned away toward the fire.

As I watched the firelight outlining her dark cloak and curved back, I thought about calling her to me, telling her what Aglaia had told me. It wasn't much, after all. Just a clue, just a hint of something more sinister than the nightmare she had already revealed. *They weren't raiders. They knew me. They knew the secret way in under the village wall.*

Oh, raiders were bad enough, and seeing your parents killed, your village ruined. How could this be worse?

But it was. I already knew that, having heard only those few words. It tasted . . . it tasted like hubris, like vengeance, like all those darker paths a life can weave. It tasted sharp and meaningful, like something you couldn't escape.

I knew that it would draw Xinot in, a mystery like that. Even I hadn't managed to keep from chasing my curiosity to the other side of Serena's spell. If my eldest sister got a whiff of what I'd found, she would want to follow this girl, all the way to the end of her thread, to let each drop of destiny soak through her limbs, slide along her bones.

Neither of my sisters was safe from this girl; I mustn't let either of them become attached. Not after Serena's children. Not after what had happened to Xinot later, out on this very island. I hadn't been able to drown Aglaia today, but I swore then that I would keep her from the others. I would take her out in the boat with me again tomorrow, and the day after that, until I could follow through with my plan of killing her at last. I would keep her bright eyes from Serena's soft heart, from Xinot's need to know.

For that night I sulked, and Xinot left me alone. I listened to Serena talking with Aglaia, and I thanked the gods for the hollowness in her cheerful replies, for the way my sister's spell had hidden the girl who had spoken to me, somewhere far below.

Four

I KEPT MY OATH; I TOOK AGLAIA OUT FISHING IN our skiff again the next morning, and then the next after that. I left the rope under my seat in the boat; each time we went, I grabbed it as soon as we were out on the waves.

But each time, I couldn't quite get my hands to tie hers. I tried using my magic; I whispered words that compel flesh to move, and my arms jerked toward the girl, and she watched patiently as I lifted her wrists. But the touch of her skin always broke my spell. I blamed it on Serena's power, twisting along the girl's arm, undoing my own magic. I never tried twice in one morning, though. As my hands fell back to my side of the boat, I dropped the rope to the floor as well. I even felt my fingers relaxing, my shoulders falling back when I reached for our lines and hooks, as if in relief.

Every morning this happened. Each day I swore fervently

that it would not happen again, and each day I was forsworn.

Those first afternoons, as I worked with my sisters on the island, I watched the girl to be sure there was no sign of the bright-gazed mortal I had seen. At least I found nothing to worry me in that. Aglaia was happy to sit in a corner much of the time, humming or sewing away at some project Serena had handed her. Sometimes she'd go on rambles around our island, leaping from rock to rock or gathering her empty stones. In the evenings after we'd eaten, she loved to sit by Serena, who would stroke the girl's hair absently. She did not bother Xinot, and my eldest sister generally behaved as though she was not there.

I kept her by my side as often as I could; I spent many hours out on our rocks with her, scaling fish or skinning vegetables. She would look out over the waves, never toward the mainland but off past the end of the island. I would listen as she began to hum her strange, haunting tunes. There were never any words in Aglaia's tunes, not any that I understood. But her singing voice was unbearably lovely, like the last lingering notes of a harp song.

One night, about a week after she'd arrived, I watched from an opposite corner of our house as Aglaia was drifting off to sleep.

We do not sleep, so we do not dream, but we have heard of the things that you mortals dream. Illusions, wrapped in longings and fears—your dreamland is a wide, dark everywhere. You do not know the things we know or taste magic on the wind. You dream, though, that you are all-powerful;

that you fly; that your lives are as important as the gods'.

Mortal dreams lie on the surface, but they tell deeper truths. As Aglaia breathed slow and slower, I watched the empty blankness that smoothed her face melt away. I saw the dreams begin to flicker across her eyes, down to twitch her mouth. She smiled, not with the perfect sweet smile she had in the daylight. She smiled small and knowingly. She frowned, as though she was thinking and as though the thinking caused her worry. She remembered.

The thoughts drained from her face, and her eyebrows drew up, her mouth opened. She did not cry out or move; the memories froze her. She wept as she dreamed; one silent, glistening tear slipped across her nose.

She knew. Even if she did not know her own name during the day, when she dreamed, she somehow knew again the horrors hidden away.

Serena was there, a shadow between me and the girl. I looked up, and she was frowning. "You mustn't watch her so, Chloe," she said. "A human's dreams are private. We've no right to see the things she dreams."

"You are right, sister," I said at once. I held out a hand, and she helped me to my feet. "We should not pry into the girl's mind. We should leave her alone."

I followed her out to the wind, and I let it tease my hair, but I did not hear the prayers it delivered; I did not feel our darkness flowing beneath my skin. There was another sound itching: it was Aglaia's soft singing, echoing here and there through my mind. I breathed in deep; my hair twisted back and my dress blew forward. But all that night I could not relax; I could not lose myself as I was used to do.

The next day, when I took Aglaia out in our skiff, I did not even try to tie her wrists. It was a brilliant blue-and-green morning; it seemed the very fish were dancing and the birds were singing paeans in the heavens. Aglaia was humming again. I sat silently, scowling.

I could hear now, even better than before, the anguished slant of her melody. It was a gentle tune, on the surface. It trilled and it soothed as did the soft-breaking sea. And she was so contented, humming it. Her hands were folded loosely, and even her hair fell gracefully down her arms and back.

But it grated against my teeth: the undercurrent, the hidden lining that glimmered if you twisted her song in just the right direction, so the light caught the thing that almost wasn't there. It was an aspen on a still day. All green, all calm—then a sudden breeze blew, and the leaves flipped, just once and then back again, but your breath had already caught at the sharp flash of silver.

With a sudden sweep of my hand near her face, I woke her. The song stopped; I could breathe.

For a few moments, we sat in silence. I had poured more strength into this untangling spell than the first one. She would remain with me for some minutes, at least. I closed my eyes, reveling in the quiet, but then I squinted them open at the girl.

She wasn't shuddering this time. The pain was there; I could see it in the jutting of her jaw, the clenching of her hands on her knees. But she was calm, and she was giving me look for look, as if waiting for some sign from me.

Oh, and I should have stayed silent. How many stories are there? About the cat who cannot help but taste the cream he knows is poisoned. The woman who cannot keep from opening the box, though she knows it will destroy the world.

You would think, after all the time we have been alive, we would have gotten over it, the wish to know, the yearning for some clue to the workings of the world. We spin it. We stretch it. We stop it short at its end—the mass of pure, dark questions at the heart of everything.

But no. The more you know, the less you understand. Questions beget questions; mysteries unfold into greater mysteries.

And curiosity never killed any immortal cat.

"Well?" I said, and she raised her eyebrows at me.

"Well?" she said.

"What is it you want? Obviously there is something."

She smiled, slightly. It was so different from the wide smile of the thoughtless girl that I went still as she started to speak.

"They all thought me so beautiful, Chloe."

"Who did?" Beyond everyone, that is.

"My parents, naturally. And everybody else's parents, and all the other girls of the village, and the boys. There used to be wagers—they'd bet real money—on who was going to win my heart. Nobody asked for my opinion; I'd have told them to save their coin for a few years yet. But nobody asked."

She let out her breath and looked away, toward the horizon.

"There were tales about me. Can you believe that? Rumors, I mean, things people would tell travelers passing through."

She stopped. She was so quiet, still turned away, that I began to think Serena's spell might have taken her. I inched toward her, only a bit. I reached out a hand; I started, "Aglaia—?"

"*Hold on*," she said, almost a snarl. I saw her face then; it wasn't a spell that had frozen her. The tears were sliding silently in tracks all down her cheeks.

When she spoke again, there was nothing calm left in her ragged voice. "The rumors must have been interesting," she said. "Because one day this great hero came all the way to our village, just to see me for himself.

"And oh, we knew of him. We knew how many monsters he had killed, how the very gods relied on him to fight their battles. There were tales of him visiting the world of the dead and coming back alive, with a bag of strange coin to prove he'd been there.

"But he seemed—to me he seemed only just another man. Handsome, yes. More in love with himself than most men. More certain that he would get his way." She paused to rub her face against her cloak.

I heard myself saying, "He wanted . . . what, to marry you?"

She nodded, and she swallowed. "That's what he said. I guess it would have been another great tale for him to win me. I didn't accept him. He wasn't kind. He didn't love me or even much care what sort of person I was."

I murmured, almost to myself, "He would not have liked that you told him no."

She replied at once, not looking at me, "Yes."

"And he came with some men to attack your village?"

"They weren't dressed as soldiers. They wore black masks and rags, and their eyes were angry."

"But you knew it was them."

"Not then. I know now. I remember the color of his face, the sound of his voice. He was there. I refused him, so he destroyed me."

She sat there, knowing the truth of it, demanding that I know it too. I didn't speak again. I didn't look at her either; I turned my face to the sun and let him play with my hair. I had asked for this. I couldn't blame the girl.

She said, "You have to help me, Chloe."

"With what?" If I closed my eyes, I could pretend she wasn't there.

For a moment I wondered if she was going to ask me to throw her from the boat, to end her pain. If she had asked, I would have done it. Every time I learned something new about this girl, she became more and more dangerous. And anyway, I told myself, most of the time she was hardly alive. It would be like putting a wingless fly out of its misery—one small squish, and she would be gone.

She didn't ask it, though. Now I know better. She never would have asked for such a thing.

She said, "You must help me find the man who did it."

"The one who led the others into your village and did those horrible things?"

"Yes," she said. "Will you help me?"

She was looking at me so directly, and through her anger and her grief, I could see her hope, clear and bright. Mortals did not look at us like that, as though we were just like them, as though we understood.

Or, only one mortal had, and he was gone.

"I know I haven't given you much to go on," Aglaia continued. "I haven't even given you his name."

"That's true," I said, grasping at it. "I don't see how I can help without a name."

"Oh!" she said, and the spell was starting to flicker now along her face. She scrunched up her eyes, concentrating: "But I do know it. . . ."

I leaned in toward her; I couldn't help myself. The whole sky was still; the whole sea was silent, waiting to see if she could dredge up the one word she thought might help.

She grabbed my arm; she pulled me even closer.

She gasped for breath, and then, her hold tightening, she had it. "Endymion," she said, so close to me. She faded, her fingers loosening, murmuring as the spell took her, "His name was Endymion."

We do not usually pay much attention to the threads we have already spun. They sit glowing on their shelves until they fizzle and fade, and are no longer there. No one threatens them; they need no guards. We do not even take them down for entertainment. A life contains a thousand stories, but we know them all. And they always end the same way: *snap*.

That evening, though, as Aglaia and Serena were boiling

vegetable soup in our cauldron, I walked along our glittering shelves, and I looked for the one he belonged to.

I found it easily. It was nearly singing my name as I passed, it was so beautiful. I reached for it.

Endymion. Such a lovely name, full of promise. A name for a young man, on the brink of life. If I had come upon this youth when we had lived in the mortal world, I would have wanted him to look at me, to see my beauty and admire it.

His thread was strong, and it shone as bright as Aglaia's. They were well-matched for each other in that. He would have been drawn to her, not only for the rumors of her looks or for the fame he could earn by winning her. He would have felt he had been walking among shadows until he saw her face.

Perhaps he mistook that brilliance for love. Or for destiny.

I placed the thread back on its shelf, and I wiped my hands on my tunic. You could not tell just by looking, but there was something twisted hidden in this young man's thread. I smelled it, a whiff of dank rot. I felt it too, prickling along my fingers.

"Chloe?"

Cold laced through me. It was Serena; I did not want her to see what was on my face.

"Yes?" I said, not turning around.

She said, "We've finished the soup. It's ready to be eaten."

"Oh," I said, and, steadying myself, "It smells divine." I looked over my shoulder and smiled at her. She was stirring the pot with one hand and tucking away a strand of Aglaia's hair with the other. She smiled back at me, my beautiful sister. There was only quiet in her eyes, only a warm contentment.

Before I went over to join them, I turned to Endymion's thread again, and I unfurled it from its coil. I measured its length, and I smiled. Then I tucked it away, against the wall at the back of the shelf. I piled several dimmer threads in front of it, though I was disappointed that his still managed to shine brightly through.

I could not help it, after that. I brought Aglaia out in the boat every morning, and each time I took away my sister's spell, watching as the girl shook away the veil, as she opened her eyes to me.

She remembered me, every time I did it. She kept asking if I would help her, and I found it harder and harder to think of what to say.

"He took everything from me, Chloe," she said one morning, and there wasn't anything hidden behind that angry voice. "All I did was tell him that I didn't want him, and he came and took it all away." She held my gaze, and I could not turn from her, could not stop her from speaking. Then she glanced out across the sea, and her face pulled in tight. It was a gloomy morning, and we were far enough out that there was no land to be seen, no rocky island or long pathway to shore. It was only us, in our little skiff, and the gray sky and the deep. She said, "I don't know . . . I don't know exactly where we are or what we are doing here. I don't mind that, somehow. But I know you, and I think that you could help me. I think that there is a power in you, Chloe."

I leaned away from her; I let my hair fall forward.

"Isn't there?" said Aglaia.

I shook my head, but somehow she knew that I wasn't saying no to her, but to the whole thing: her pleas for help, her insistence that I could, her need for it.

"Yes, there is," she said. "I can see it in your face, even when you hide away like that. You're looking at me out of the corners of your eyes, but it glints there, still. It's a dark sort of thing that lives in you. I sometimes think that if you stepped out of this boat, you could walk across the waves, or you could step up into the sky."

I laughed, thinking of what the sun would say. "I couldn't do that."

"But you could do something."

"No," I insisted. "There is nothing I can do."

She sighed, and she wrinkled her nose, turning from me.

After such conversations, I rowed us back to shore convinced that I would never talk to her again, though that did not last long. What did last was my certainty that I could not let my sisters see the Aglaia that I knew. Once or twice as I was spinning, I almost let it get to me. I'd think about the life that had been granted this girl, the path she'd been made to walk. We had given her that path—we and the mystery we served. We had led Aglaia to tragedy, to loss. My skin would prickle as I reached for my wool. I'd want to drop it, to stab at it with my spindle, to tear it into little bits and let it drift away across the sea.

I'd want to punish it, the thing that had hurt Aglaia so.

No, I told my wool as it itched against my palms. *No, I am not concerned with that girl. No, I will not fail you, not today, not tomorrow. I have not the weakness of my sisters.*

I gritted my teeth, and I kept at my work.

It soon enough seemed that the problem was solving itself. As one week drew into two, and two to three, I found that Aglaia's moments of clarity were growing shorter, no matter how much effort I put into my spell.

She didn't talk as much about Endymion or the raiders; she stopped asking for my help so frequently. Instead her thoughts seemed to be focused more and more on the early days of her childhood: She spoke of her mother teaching her to bake bread, of harvesting the fields with her father, of playing games with her brother and sister.

On one of the last days that Aglaia and I went out in the boat, she told me a story from the very beginning of her life, when her parents had taken her to visit a local oracle.

"It was the tradition," she said. She was murmuring that morning, drifting halfway between Serena's spell and her waking self. She spoke almost in one sentence, long and meandering like our boat's path through the waves. I was listening quietly, my hands laid light along the sides of the boat.

"The oracle gives most babies in our village the same blessing," Aglaia went on. "A long, happy life. She gave my parents that blessing, when they were born, and my brother and my sister, too.

"Sometimes she mixes it up. She says one or two of our children will have problems to overcome, that their roads will not be all easiness and comfort. She never says, though, that they'll not win out in the end, and those who receive this harder blessing take it as a challenge. When they find themselves in difficulty, they tell their neighbors, 'Thus the oracle said that it would be,' and they do not despair over their fate. They take heart in its inevitability and fight through to happier days."

I could see today's clarity fading already, the light, pale as it was, diminishing in her eyes. I was struck with a sudden premonition that I would not speak to her in this meandering way again. These long mornings in the boat were drawing to a close; after this, the spell would take her.

I had to keep her here just a few minutes longer. I had to hear the end of this story; I had to know Aglaia's fate—whether it was the long, happy life or the harder blessing. I reached across and took her hands, held them tight. She blinked down at them.

"What did the oracle say about you, Aglaia?" I asked her. I didn't think it would be anything true; such women are almost all of them faking their powers for status in the villages they serve or for a few extra coins.

Aglaia blinked, and blinked again. "She said . . ."

I gripped her hands harder. "What?"

Her face snapped clear for an instant and she said, looking straight at me, "She gave me three words that she said would shape the course of my life. The first was *beauty*; my parents smiled at that." I did too. Anyone with eyes could have given her that fortune. "The second was *clarity*, a vision of the world not skewed by any illusion. The third . . ." She trailed off again, shaking her head.

I was frowning. *Clarity?* What sort of oracle gave that word to a child, and one who was destined to grow so clear-eyed as this girl, so true and purposeful? "What was it?" I said. I squeezed Aglaia's hands. "What was the third word?"

She kept shaking her head. "I don't know." Her hold was slackening. Her voice was softening. "My parents never would tell me what the third word was. They used to look at each other, though, when I asked. They looked at each other . . . I could see . . ."

She shut her eyes. When she opened them, she would be gone.

"Aglaia?" I leaned in close to her, murmuring the words and sending them softly to her ears so it would sound as if they came from inside her own head. "What did you see?"

She said, only a whisper, trailing off into nothing, "When my parents looked at each other, I could see their fear."

Then she let go of my hands, and she opened her eyes to me. She tilted her head, blinking, smiling prettily.

Five

I SHOULD HAVE KNOWN BETTER. HADN'T THERE been enough warnings? It hadn't only been Serena's children—even here, even out at the edge of the world, the danger had come to find us, long before this mortal girl showed up. And oh, it hadn't been some hero come to beg for the answer to a riddle, and it hadn't been some god's son completing an impossible task. The most dangerous things—do you know this yet?—the most dangerous things are small and harmless. They look at you out of their bright round eyes, and they rub your ankles with their soft round heads. The most dangerous things worm their way inside of you, until you forget what you've always loved, until you betray what you've always believed in.

The night after Aglaia told me of her prophecy, I stood out with my sisters at the edge of our shore. I watched Serena's moon gleam; I listened to our waves crash. I tried to understand how I could have let myself become so involved with this girl.

I had felt our magic gathering around her, and I had heard her story, the powerful tragedy of her path. I had grappled with it as we worked—the thought that Aglaia's horror had been shaped at my spindle. The thread had prickled against my palms, but I had managed it. I had been sure that our camaraderie, our acquaintanceship—whatever it was—held no real danger.

But I had been wrong. I knew it now, because when I had heard Aglaia's prophecy—beauty, clarity, and something so terrifying her parents had never told her what it was—I had not shrugged it off. I had not reasoned that the oracle was surely false. I had not reminded myself that thus were the lives of mortals: unpreventable, tragic more times than not.

I had been willing, in just that moment, to destroy the whole tangle of the web we spun, if I could set Aglaia free.

Out there, under the shifting stars, I grappled with my anger one more time; I faced it head on, feeling its broken edges.

Give me someone to love, a young girl's voice begged, blowing on a breeze.

And another, *I think that he loves me. How can I be sure?*

And a third, *The world is ours, it seems. Let us keep this happiness. Let us be together.*

My pleading girls, my young ones . . . there are some mortal women who pray to us, as they would to gods. We have no real influence over their lives, but they look to us for guidance anyway, and we hear their whispers on the winds that sweep all about our island. The young girls, just beginning to round themselves out, send their prayers to me. The mothers talk to Serena, and the old ones, with all their wisdom gnarling their hands and teeth, make their requests to Xinot.

The whispers of my girls that night were so concerned with love. They had no thread to spin, no darkness to serve. When their love was lost, they could rage without fear. If the one they loved fell into some great tragedy, they could go mad if they wished, and the world would keep on turning.

My sisters were looking out to sea, their hair drifting gently. I closed my eyes, and I listened to the thrumming underneath, the beating heart of our magic. For the first time in many days, I let it fill me up. It was a pattern old as starlight, a marvel old as time.

My anger slipped away; the prayers whispered along my cheeks, lifting away the tears I could not help in that moment, knowing how close I had come, knowing how much I had almost betrayed. I loved my sisters; I loved my work. Aglaia was new, unknown, mortal. Next to our glory, she was nothing.

I determined then, finally and certainly, that I would not speak to her anymore. I would let the spell take her deeper away from herself. She would disappear, and I would not think of her again.

Oh, and it would have worked; she would have faded, and I never would have thought of her, or only at intervals, as a strange memory, a danger that had come in on the tide and had gone away again.

A week passed. I fished from the shore. I did not go out in the boat, and when Xinot asked me why, I said I was growing bored with spending so much time with our blank-faced guest. She did not question it. She had forgotten, I think, the darkness gathering; she had forgotten the moment that first night when Serena's spell had flickered and a piece of the truth had shown itself on the girl's face.

She had forgotten, or she had decided not to think of it again. I took her example, and I put the last weeks' discoveries from my mind. Aglaia, the one I knew, the one who told me secrets and looked at me with hope, was gone. The girl on our island was only a shell, an empty flask, a rained-out cloud shredding itself to bits.

It should have been obvious, the thing that pulled Aglaia back to us.

Any mortal woman would have noticed long ago, but we aren't alive enough to have felt it ourselves. And by the time I realized, Aglaia knew as well. She *knew*. She didn't have a bit of sense left in her, but she would trail her fingers across her belly. She wouldn't be looking at anything in particular, but there was purpose in her eyes again. There was sharpness, even as they went all soft around the edges.

I saw it before my sisters did. It had been several days since I had last taken Aglaia out in the boat, and they hardly noticed her anymore, she was so hollow. She gathered her stones and sang her songs; she slept and she ate. They could ignore her as they ignored a flock of birds overhead or a creeping plant covering a rock.

But I still watched her, now and again. I saw the hand on her belly, the focus in her gaze. When I thought, I knew that she hadn't bled, and it had been five weeks since she arrived; the moon had waxed and waned. How utterly blind we had been.

A baby could not be ignored; a baby could not be forgotten. I knew that I could not hide this secret from my sisters for long.

Before I told them, though, I took Aglaia out in the boat once more and passed my hand across her face.

She looked up at me at once. It was the old Aglaia, just as much *there* as she had been the first time, when she had told me that the raiders hadn't been raiders at all.

"Chloe," she said, certain, "I am going to have a baby."

"Yes, I know." I had to ask it. "Was there a man that you loved in your village? Were you about to be married?"

She turned her gaze toward her belly. She shook her head. "No. There was no one."

"There must have been someone."

"No."

She looked back up at me, frowning. I knew. I had known before I asked, but I hadn't wanted to believe it.

Already, she was fading again. I hadn't put much effort into my spell; all I had needed was the answer to that one thing.

"Chloe," Aglaia said urgently, reaching across and grasping

my hand. As she had so many times before, she begged, "You must help me."

And I answered, once again, "There is nothing I can do."

But in between the flickerings of Serena's spell, her eyes were wider and clearer than I had ever seen them, and her cheeks were flushed with more than the brisk sea breeze. "Chloe," she pleaded, "I don't know where I am. I don't know where I am going to be in the next several months or if I am going to be able to care for myself. And Chloe, I am going to have a *baby*."

She fought the spell as it took her. I saw the struggle there on her face, and I couldn't look away from her. She had never battled with it like this. When it had come before, it had been between one blink and the next, and she had gone quietly into its hold. Now I could see my Aglaia still there, even as her eyes glazed, even as her breaths smoothed. She was there, just behind it, and she held on, one moment, two, with nothing but the jagged fingernails of her will.

It took her, though, in the end. And then she was sitting all placid again, and I was alone in the boat.

I told my sisters that evening after we'd eaten, while Aglaia was out gathering her stones. There really was no point in keeping this a secret. It was better to tell them at once, before they discovered it for themselves.

We were in our usual places around the fire: Xinot on her stump, Serena leaning back in her chair. I hadn't ever reclaimed my stool from Aglaia after that first night. I used it while we worked with our threads during the day, but once the sun had fallen, I left it for the girl and sat on the floor. It had suited me, anyway. Because I was below the others, they saw fewer of the glances I shot our guest, less of whatever worry I couldn't hide away.

I was braiding a basket that evening for gathering our vegetables. I'd snipped its long grasses from along our northern shore. They bent when I told them to bend, and when they dried, they held their form perfectly.

The wind was rushing outside our open door. There was a green cast to the sky; it would storm before the night was through.

My sisters stared at me, Serena's hand going to her mouth and Xinot, for a moment, speechless in her shock.

"A *baby*?" said Serena.

Xinot echoed her. "She's going to have a baby?"

"Who is the father?" said Serena.

"Was she married?" said Xinot. "She didn't say anything about a husband, did she?"

"No," said Serena, "we would have remembered that. Maybe there was a sweetheart, maybe from another village. He could still be alive."

"And we've been keeping her from him."

Serena stood, her eyes wide. "I have to take the spell away. We have to send her back."

I kept my head down; I kept on plaiting the grasses for our basket.

"She has a life, after all," Serena continued. "She has that whole long thread." She looked over at its shelf; we all knew exactly where Aglaia's thread lived. I had caught both of my sisters standing beside it in the first few weeks after the girl arrived, watching it gleam. They never touched it, though. Neither did I, nor did I search for its coil in my mind and read it there. I'd no wish to know any more of this girl's path than I already did.

"So she'll raise the child," Xinot said. "It doesn't need us."

Without looking up, without pausing in my plaiting, I snapped, "Of course it doesn't need us. It's a human baby. It's nothing to do with us."

"Yes, of course," said Serena. "She should go back to the father, anyway. She would want that."

I agreed with Serena. The girl should go. Still, I couldn't help saying, "We don't know if the father lives. He might have died in the raid."

"Maybe. But what if he didn't? What if he's been mourning her all this time?"

I didn't answer. My hair was all about me, a pall keeping out the light. The first of the raindrops were beginning to splatter onto our roof; far-off thunder threatened. I could smell the grasses crinkling as I tucked them tight, one over the other over the other.

A finger poked through into my sight. It was gnarled, crooked. It swept back a length of my hair, and one swirling eye peered in. "Chloe," Xinot said, "you have always wanted to send her back."

I glared out at my sister. "I *do* want to send her back." She was overlooking the obvious. They both were, but I'd have expected Xinot to catch on more quickly than this.

She saw the certain knowledge on my face, and the eye whirled and deepened. She drew back.

When she spoke, it was cold. "The father wasn't a villager, Serena. He was a raider."

A sharp tongue of lightning licked our walls, and then I heard my kindest sister sitting abruptly in her chair. The grasses went one over the other over the other. Xinot poked at the fire with her stick; my hair shone orange at the edges, and the end of my nose began to warm.

They didn't ask me how I knew. They didn't question the statement's truth. We know truth; we know its shape and texture, and they could not help but believe me.

The splattering turned to a steady, hard rhythm and then merged into one heavy sound. The water was starting to come in through our door, but none of us moved to shut it. After a minute, Aglaia came rushing in, her pockets full of stones, soaked through. She shut the door and greeted us as she always did, bright, vague. She didn't seem to notice when none of us replied.

"We'll keep it, then," said Serena, as Aglaia went over to her blankets to deposit her loot and then took up her position on my stool, wringing her hair. The storm had arrived in truth now: The lightning flickered across our faces, turning them eerie as a mortal's dream. We spoke between cracks of thunder.

"We can't," I said, through clenched teeth.

I heard Serena drawing in a breath, low, harsh. She spoke in the same tone: "You saw her when she arrived, Chloe. You know what pain the girl was in. We can't give her back to that."

Yes, I had seen her. Yes, I knew Aglaia's pain, and I knew the fire in her eyes as she begged me for help.

Snap. The grass I had been weaving was broken to bits in my hand. I said, irritated, tossing the basket from my lap, "We cannot raise a child, Serena!"

Aglaia looked over at me. The basket had tumbled into the fire, and the glow from its sudden flame caught in her hair, swept along her cheeks. "A child?" she said. "Is someone going to have a baby?" Her voice was as light as ever, but I saw the hand that drifted to her stomach; I saw how it hovered there, protecting.

This time, my sisters saw it too.

"She knows," Xinot muttered.

"Only deep inside of her," I said, frozen, watching the girl. "Not on the surface."

Xinot's mouth narrowed. "Not yet."

Serena was watching Aglaia with some strange question, as though she'd never seen this girl before, as though she was noticing the color of her eyes for the first time, the shape of her arms, the curve of her neck. "Aglaia," she said, soft as a bird's belly, "do you like children?"

Aglaia's face brightened, as a small girl's does on hearing some happy news. "I love children," she said. She leaned over toward my sister, her hand still placed on her dress, gentle. "Do you have children?" She looked about at us all. "I think that you do, or you will. I think there are going to be children."

Xinot stood abruptly, and Aglaia startled, staring up at her. "Serena," my sister said, "you cannot protect her from this."

Serena's face gleamed; she rubbed a hand across it and stood as well, turning from Aglaia. "No," she said. "I'll have to bring her back."

They looked down at me, still crouched across the fire from the girl. The way she had her face turned up toward my sisters, the trust that shone through her—she wouldn't look at us like this again.

But of course we had to do it. I *wanted* to do it. We would finally be getting rid of her. I pushed myself up from the floor and shook my tunic out so it fell full about my ankles. I threw my hair back. I met my sisters' gazes. "Yes," I said as the thunder rumbled beneath. "It is time."

Six

WE PULLED AGLAIA TO HER FEET AND LED HER
over to the front of the house. We ranged ourselves before
her, as we had been when she had first appeared on our
island. Me, then Serena, then Xinot—all facing the girl, who
stood with her back to our door as though she had entered
only a few moments ago.

Serena stepped up next to her. She held Aglaia's hand and
slid her other one behind the girl's head, over her hair, and
she whispered something in her ear. I saw Aglaia's face as the
spell came away. It wasn't the smooth, sudden understanding in our boat. This jerked her; this made her cry out with
its shock, and when Serena backed away, Aglaia was looking
about at us with wild eyes.

This was not the Aglaia that I knew.

Oh, there were similarities. As she caught my gaze, I saw the same stubbornness and the same spark. Her posture was the same—tall, confident. But the light in her eyes, the strength of her presence were stunning. As the spellbound Aglaia was only an echo of the girl in the boat, so that girl was only an echo of this one.

And she didn't know me.

That was her first question, in fact, when she was able to speak. "Who are you?"

There was no way that we could not answer. We told her our names.

"Those are just names," said Aglaia. "Who are you?"

Serena turned to Xinot; Xinot turned to me. I said, a whisper, not looking at her, "We're the shadow behind the stars."

She must have followed my gaze, because she walked over to my basket of wool and my spindle. Xinot made some gesture toward her, but Aglaia didn't try to touch either. She just looked at them, straight and still.

She said, slow, remembering, "I came to ask you what there was to live for now."

Yes, we said.

"You wouldn't answer me."

No.

She said, and it was small and breaking, "What did you do to me?"

Serena moved over beside her. She reached out to take the girl's hand, but then dropped hers again. "We took away your pain."

"No." Aglaia was shaking her head. "It never went away."

"It did. You smiled. You were happy."

"I was happy, maybe, but I was still in pain." She looked at Serena. There was no wild panic now, only certainty. "I can feel the place where it's been living. It never went away."

She looked down at my wool again. "You did this thing," she said. "You brought the doom upon my village; you gave this pain to me."

"It wasn't us," said Serena.

"We only listen to the thread," said Xinot.

I was silent. Of course the girl was right.

Aglaia turned; she crossed in front of us and went up close to Xinot. "You cut their threads. My mother. My father. Everyone."

She went up close to Serena. "You showed her where to cut."

She came up close to me, and I shuddered at the lack of recognition in her face. All those mornings out in the boat, all those words we had exchanged, and there was nothing left. Not even memory.

Then, though, before she spoke, she blinked, and I saw the hesitation there, and I saw my Aglaia, the one who had held my hand, begging me to help her, there in her bright-blue eyes. She said softly, "You spun them such threads as would lead them to that day."

Xinot tried to reason with her. "It wasn't our fault, child. We didn't know."

"You knew," said Aglaia, and her voice was hard again.

She turned to our eldest sister and pointed a finger, sure and strong. "You *knew*. Are you going to tell me that when you spin and measure and cut, you've no idea what you are doing? Are you going to tell me that you cannot hear the threads singing, telling you their tales? *I* hear them. I've spent so long in your hovel, and so empty, that their songs have crept in under my skin." She stopped; she closed her eyes. "I can hear them now, at the edges of my mind, murmuring to me. Are you going to tell me, sisters, that you hear less than I do?"

We had pulled together, Xinot, Serena, and I. We had stepped away from her as she spoke, linking our arms, becoming one. We knew one another's thoughts, and we knew how little we wanted to say this thing. But we deal in truth. Beginning, middle, or end: We could not tell this girl a falsehood any more than we could have given her family different births or lives or deaths.

We know, we said. *We know the song of the thread as we know our own fingers, our own palms. We have only to shut our eyes to read any thread we choose.*

"Yes," said Aglaia. "I know you can. I know you do."

How many nights had we sat with this girl around our fire? How many times had she laughed with us, and now it was as though she had never heard our voices, had never kissed our cheeks before she snuggled into her blankets.

She turned from us without saying another word. She took her cloak down from its peg. She stepped through our door out into the rain, and the wind threw it shut behind her.

~

It stormed all that night and into the next day. We did not go out to the sea; we did not do our work. We sat around our fire and watched the lightning's shadow sliding along our threads, sparking them orange and red and white. We listened to the thunder; we felt the rain hurling itself along our roof, a loud, messy drumbeat. It raged, this storm, a tearing, howling thing. It did not want to leave the world the way it was. It wanted to bite and thrash. It wanted to destroy.

The fire did little that night to diminish the dark that had trickled in under our walls, through the cracks at the edges of our door. It was a dense darkness, alive and certain. It had come when Serena had taken her spell from the girl, as though it had been waiting, as though Aglaia was a scented flower and it an eager bee.

We knew it. Not only because it was ours—it was our magic—but we knew this particular darkness, this thing that had shaped her path. We knew it because it was *hers*. Aglaia had said that when she closed her eyes, she could feel our threads murmuring to her, that she had spent so long in our house that our magic had begun to creep in under her skin. Aglaia had been empty; that had allowed our magic in. But we are also empty, in a way. It's why we go out to the waves every night—to fill ourselves back up. And living with this girl for so many weeks, I think something similar had happened with us and her powerful fate.

I knew my sisters could feel it too. We could hear one another breathing, and we knew the tingle that was inching along every bit of us. I had been right to keep this girl from them. One conversation, one look at the true Aglaia, and they could not look away again.

We resisted it, all through that night and half the day, as the storm barked and snarled. We tried to forget the shine of her eyes. We tried to ignore the dark undercurrent swirling around our ankles, singing to us as a siren would, to come, to jump, to dive.

I tried to remember my determination that I would let this girl go.

When the thunder had rolled away, when the lightning had paled and then diminished, the darkness still churned, and our breaths still caught, and we still tingled.

The gulls began to call out to one another, asking how their neighbors had fared through the rain. I left my sisters sitting silent, and I went to our door and pushed at it. It complained, but I snapped a word, and the door flew open, and the world rushed in.

The sea was rolling and rolling, energized from the storm. The air was cool and buoyant. Even through the clouds, the sun reached down pale tendrils, gleaming at the ends of my hair, pulling me toward him, murmuring my name.

I followed; I went out past our house to the east end of the island, where a line of rocks led me out to a point overlooking the frantic waves.

I stood there in the final drizzle, the winds whipping round. I closed my eyes against them; the sun touched my lids with soft gray kisses, and the sea showered me with spray.

Of all us sisters I am the most susceptible to sensory

passion—for a human boy who fetches us water from a well; for a poem; for a place. Not the comforting love of Serena's mothering, but a hard, fiery love that tears at the space where I would keep a soul.

I gave myself up to it, standing there. I took in the sea and the sky; I let the sun flatter me. If I stood like this long enough, I might forget Aglaia's words about it being our fault. I might forget the tug of her thread, the smell of it, the shine. I might forget the baby and Endymion and the way she said my name. *Chloe*, she used to say. *Chloe, you must help me.*

When I went back along the line of rocks toward our house, I saw what the storm had done to our garden. The leaves were bruised; the stalks were bent. The peas, the beans were scattered like so much bird food. And our vines.

Serena had come out of the house as well; she was standing next to what was left of them. Tiny grapes had squished, here and there, in the melee. Our trellises were broken into fragments. Grape leaves draped over every bit of the garden, and the vines were tangled strings.

I went over to my sister and I touched her arm. "They weren't much to speak of, anyway."

She shook her head. One hand was near her mouth, and she stared down at the mess as though there was nothing else.

"We'll plant new ones. We'll do it better; they'll grow tall and beautiful. You'll see."

"Oh, Chloe," she murmured. "Do you think I care about the vines?"

"Don't you?"

She shook her head again.

"What is it, then?"

She turned to look at me. The sky was in her eyes. "He used to sit here. Right here. He used to bat at the fruit and watch the birds fly."

That creature, the one who had wormed his way into our lives. It was hard to tell, with everything all over the place. But she was right. Just here was where he used to sit, and just here was where we buried him. And the storm had covered it over with vines and sticks and small squished grapes.

I got down on my knees and reached out a hand to the muddle, swept away some leaves. After a moment, Serena folded herself to kneel beside me. As the clouds started to peel away and a fresh new breeze came in, we cleared the mess from the creature's grave, until the dirt was bare and the fallen vines formed a wreath.

Then I sat back on my heels as Serena bent over it, her face hidden behind her hair as mine so often was.

I watched her, and I smelled this breeze, and I smelled Aglaia's thread, and I thought.

This girl was so dangerous. Her path might lead us any-where, to any sort of terrible place. Already even I had lost faith in our work, questioning the rightness of her fate.

If we left, I still would not be able to risk telling my sisters the dark secrets she had told me. I alone would have to know what Aglaia had said. I would have to bear it, and not let even my face show it.

I don't know how Xinot came up behind us so silently,

but then again, I don't know why I was surprised that she could. She bent her craggy face down near my shoulder and said, "Can you smell it, Chloe? The future that sparks on this wind?" She turned her nose into it, looking out to sea, and then swiveled her neck so she was facing our rocky path and the mainland. The breeze was sweeping just like that, in from the sea, over our rocks toward land. Of course there were no actual sparks, but it did smell as though there were: sharp and exciting, new as my wool.

It was pushing at us, and Aglaia's thread was pulling at us, and my sister's eyes were whirling.

Xinot reached behind her back, and she dragged two large black sacks around to me. I peered into them.

"I don't know . . . ," I said.

She slipped a small purse out from her skirt. It jangled, and Serena looked up, over at her. "This is for you, sister," Xinot said, and thrust the bag into Serena's hands. "I'll have enough to do pulling my old bones along."

Serena opened her bag as well, though we all knew what it was. When we had come away from the mainland, we had brought quite a stash of coin with us. We'd tucked the bits into the corners of our house; while Serena and I cleared the vines, Xinot must have been hobbling from wall to wall, finding our pieces. The coin wouldn't be what they used today, but it was gold.

Serena said, with such hope that I knew it was already far too late, "Are we going to follow her?"

Xinot pointed her cane into the wind. "I'm not entirely sure we have a choice. You can feel the strength of this thing as well as I can." She peered closely at us. "You can *smell* it."

I was shaking my head. "I don't know . . ."

Serena murmured, tying the bag closed, "She shines bright."

Xinot tilted her head. "She pulls dark."

I did try. I said, "She's nothing to do with us," but even I didn't believe it when I said it.

My eldest sister shrugged. "Suit yourself." She held out a hand to Serena. "Coming?"

Serena didn't take the hand, but she pushed herself to her feet. "We can't go without Chloe."

"Nonsense." Xinot took Serena's arm. Much too effectively for a woman her age, she pulled our sister away, to the west, toward the pathway leading to the mainland.

As they left the grassy green cap of our island and started down the rocks, Serena was still protesting, and Xinot was still pointing her nose ahead determinedly, pushing away with her cane. I called out to them, "Wait!"

Xinot kept on, but Serena tugged at her arm. They stopped at the edge of the rocky pathway, looking back at me.

"Just—wait," I called. I picked up one of the big black packs, and I ran back into our house.

Xinot had filled one bag with my spindle and wool; the other, the one I carried now, was mostly empty, for whatever threads we spun along the way. It held only one thing: a coil of long, golden thread, glittering bright as day.

I walked along our shelves, listening for the other. It was as easy to find as it had been before, and I slipped it into the bag, though I didn't like to see it curling up next to hers.

Then I tied the sack shut, and I slipped its strap over my head, across one shoulder. It was light; the other would be much heavier. I took my cloak down from its peg and grabbed Serena's as well. Xinot was wearing hers already; she rarely took it off.

I hesitated before I opened the door.

What were we doing? How did we think we could follow a mortal girl, no matter how strong the pull of her thread, no matter how the wind sparked? What did we think we were going to do if we found her at the end of this path? We were not the sort who did things. We were what *is*, what *must be*, what *cannot be altered*. We were not meant to meddle.

I shut my eyes, and I tried to remember, again, all the reasons I had decided to let Aglaia go, all the reasons there were to be glad that we were alone on our island once more.

But there, behind my eyelids, was the girl's bright face. There was the sky in my sister's eyes as she stood by our creature's grave. And there was the coil of Aglaia's thread, calling, teasing, tempting me to go, to leap, to dive.

I was drawn by her path, and my sisters were drawn as moths to a flame, as ravens to a shine.

Even if I went out to them now and said that I couldn't come, it was possible that Xinot would shrug her bony shoulders and turn her rounded back, and she would leave anyway. And where Xinot went, Serena would go. And what was I to do: spin my thread and hand it off to no one? Listen to the prayers on the wind without my sisters there beside me?

Without one another, we are nothing. Not mortals, not gods. Empty, lonely voices swallowed up by the world.

I passed through our door, and I shut it tight behind me. I whispered a good-bye to my sea and my winds. The sun would never leave me, but the others were keening when I turned my back to them.

I went around to the garden and picked up my other pack. My sisters were still waiting at the edge of the rocks climbing to the mainland. Serena smiled as I came up next to them, and Xinot gave me a nod and a twitch of her eyebrows. I nodded back, though I had no answering grin. I hefted my packs more securely, and I followed them from our island.

PART TWO

Seven

THERE HAD BEEN A CAT.

Maybe you have already figured this out—that the creature we had buried beneath our vines, the creature who first brought us such danger, had been sweet and soft and helpless.

I have not told you much of him yet; it hasn't been important to our story. But the thread is unwinding now toward the world's end, and you will need to know this soon enough. So I will need to speak of it, much as it hurts me to say it. There will be more hurting later; I will think of this as practice.

It had been Xinot who found him, wandering through a storm out along our rocky path; and Monster had always been Xinot's cat, before he was Serena's, before he was mine. Serena wouldn't have had it in her not to love a fluffy bit of a kitten. But there was also something mysterious about him, so as to enrapture my eldest sister. Monster had never seemed to me an ordinary cat.

Maybe it was how close he had come to death that day—he was so small, and so ill-fed, that surely he would have been swept off to sea in that storm if Xinot hadn't brought him home. After that, he was always loyal to her, though Serena rubbed his ears most often and I caught his fish. Xinot was as likely to ignore him as to invite him onto her lap, but he would sit by her side anyway, most nights, no matter how Serena tried to coax him.

And he did not fear. Not the jagged spaces between our rocks, not the hawks and terns many times larger than him. He even went roaming for his mice through thunderstorms as dreadful as the one that had brought him to us. As the lightning flashed sharpest, he'd show up at our door, bedraggled and shedding lakes. His eyes would be bright; his tail would lash. While the raindrops pounded against our roof, he'd jump at the shadows like a kitten, even when he was many years old. The gods have decreed that cats will hate water, but Monster came alive in a storm. It seemed the closer he was to death—sharp rocks, grasping claws, and especially the near drowning of his childhood—the more delighted he became.

Is it any wonder, then, that Xinot loved him?

For many years, Monster was as essential a part of our lives as our piles of thread, as our spindle and shears, as our nights at the edge of the waves. Maybe, for a while, even I thought he would stay forever. Maybe we began to believe that he had come to us because he really was no ordinary cat, and that he would live as long as we did, as long as the stars still burned.

Sometimes we are as hopeless as you mortals, with your impossible dreams. Sometimes even we blind ourselves, as though the world stops spinning when we can't see.

Oh, nothing especially horrible happened to our Monster. Nothing more horrible than happens every day to thousands of cats. He was old. He had lived with us longer than most cats are granted life. When he grew sick, we knew that the end would be coming soon. We built him a bed of blankets by our fire, and we took him outside to see the sky each night, to watch the waves coming in. He was not unhappy.

Until the end, my sisters did not grieve. Xinot sat beside the cat many hours of each day; our work went on as always, but at a slower pace. I have never seen my eldest sister touch anything as gently as she touched Monster's fur, between his ears, down the curve of his back, out to the end of his tail. Again and again she would stroke him, and she would whisper a deep, soft tune that made his eyes twitch and his legs stretch out.

When she stood up, she grimaced, holding her back and rubbing her shoulders, but never once did she complain of pain.

Serena—she was all smiles and busyness as Monster faded away. She started coming out to fish with me, though the cat was losing his appetite and most of what we caught went to waste. The fish he did eat, Serena ground to a soft paste. As she slipped it between his jaws, she chattered to him of the color of the sea today, of the birds we'd seen out on the rocks, who would have fled for their lives if Monster had been on one of his stalks.

When Monster stopped swallowing the food Serena fed him, she took to sitting next to Xinot, reaching out now and again to touch his head as well.

I watched them. From across the room, I watched their little trio, and I was glad my sisters were not despairing over their pet. I didn't join them in their vigil. I did bring in a toy mouse I had made for Monster out of wood and soft bird feathers, which he kept tucked between some stones at the back of our house. I put it near his nose, where he could smell it, and I scratched his ears. When we knew it would only be hours now and the others were out of the house for a moment, I came over again and bent down near him. "Little Monster," I said, "we are going to miss you dreadfully. Go well into the dark."

Then I kissed him, right at the top of his head. He made a soft mewing noise, so I knew that he knew I was there.

When my sisters came back inside, I was against the opposite wall, and I didn't come back over until he had reached the end of his thread.

There are only so many places on our island with dirt soft enough for digging, and we talked about taking him out in our skiff and giving him a burial at sea. But none of us could bear the thought of him drowning out there forever, his fur going slick and his lungs filling up.

Instead we dug a spot for him under the grapevines, where

he had liked to bat at our tiny fruit and flatten himself against the trellises, watching for gulls.

When that was done, Serena and Xinot turned from the grave, their faces blank as the dull gray sky, and went back into the house. I came inside after them; they had already sat on their stump and chair facing the door, Xinot with her scissors out, Serena turned toward my basket as if waiting for me to hand her the next thread.

I didn't say anything. Maybe they wished to forget themselves in their work, to think of anything but the way Monster's eyes had closed and his frame had shuddered as he went. I couldn't blame them for that. I took up my usual spot, and soon my spindle was whirring.

Almost right away I knew that something was wrong.

As I passed the start of our thread to Serena, I noticed the first of the signs—her fingers curled just a tad differently than usual, just a smidgen less elegantly, so that as she pulled the thread across her palm, it grated. Not as a rough spoon against a pan; not as a harsh crow call in the morning. As a grain of sand in a lump of butter, maybe, or a tiny speck in a bowl of pure cream.

But this was already much worse than Serena's tense silence on the mainland. This was enough to slow the thread down. I spun at my usual speed—I know no other. And Serena took the thread almost as quickly, almost as smoothly. But not quite. Instead of clarity and ease, I felt a strange tightness growing in my hands. I ignored it. I kept on with my work; I tried to slow the spindle, without any success. Serena passed the thread and marked the place for Xinot's scissors.

I heard the blades opening. My spinning stopped. I looked over at my sisters, jolted out of my work by a sudden dread. Xinot's blades did not sound like that. They were not supposed to *scream* as they opened.

Xinot was glowering at the thread, as though she hated it, as though she blamed it for something. Serena's face was expressionless, as if all her joy in our work had been extinguished. She was still handing the thread to Xinot, marking it with her nails. It was wrong, the place she'd marked. I could feel the thread twisting and shivering, and I could smell it smoldering, red-hot in its wrongness.

It was not a death. I could not think to know precisely which, but it was much too short or much too long—either way, disaster; either way, a world's end.

I could not move. I could only watch as this angered Xinot took the thread, as her scissors straddled the place the joyless Serena had marked. She would know better. That was surely why I was pausing so long. I was certain that my eldest sister would be able to feel the wrongness too. But there was nothing stopping her for several long heartbeats—nothing until I gave a great gasp and threw myself toward her.

I snatched the thread away. Her scissors *snapped* on empty air.

We stared at one another. Serena blinked, and a bit of light came back into her face. The fury on Xinot's faded just a shade.

In the calm, we knew how close we had come to something

terrible. The darkness was swirling all about us; we could taste our magic, as we can on starlit nights. It was filling us up, so that our fingers buzzed with its mystery. Our eyes shone, in fear.

The darkness does not speak to us in words. There are some human oracles who claim to hear its voice. Perhaps they do, or perhaps they interpret the sensations of the dark, translate its deeper stirrings into human speech. We need no such translation. Our magic was warning us. It was telling us that the balance of the world had nearly tipped, and that it would have been our fault.

It was pouring horror into us. It was showing us the whole tangled web of its power, as though we did not already know its shape and complexity. It was reminding us of our purpose, and we were remembering our love of it, how unthinkable it would be to unravel one strand of its maze.

I dropped the thread, and it coiled back onto my spindle. The darkness drifted away.

"Chloe," Serena said at last. I did not look at her. I was shaking. "I am sorry," she said. "I could not help it. It was our magic that took him away." She sounded lost, but I could not comfort her.

I didn't care how upset they were. Nothing excused putting at risk everything we loved. How could they? It was too precious; it was too beautiful; it was too *alive*.

"Just a cat," I said after a moment, and I could not keep my voice calm. I could not keep the tears away, and I hoped my sisters realized they were tears of rage—that I wasn't like them, that I could never be as weak as them. "He was just a *stupid* cat."

No, I wouldn't think of him. I wouldn't remember his fur beneath my fingers or the sweetness of his voice.

Xinot said, into the tight, hard silence, "We will not work today."

It was practical. It could have been nothing more than an assurance that we would not mess it up again. But her words had been harsher than that, with more of a snarl. She had heard our magic as clearly as I had, and she had felt it urging us to accept the rightness of our threads. Xinot was saying that at least for today she would do no such thing.

The wisest, the darkest of my sisters, refusing to accept death. And the kindest, the most comforting of them, asking me for understanding. My horror had not left with the darkness. They were turning their backs on our magic, so I turned my back to them, and I left the house and the island to take our boat out alone as far as I could go. I did not answer when the sun spoke my name; I did not look into the waves to see what deep creatures might be somersaulting. I only rowed as hard as I could, and the tears fell hot along my cheeks, and I hated my sisters, that day, for what they had almost betrayed.

We did no work that day, nor all that night. We picked up the threads again the next morning, and Serena's face was calm and bright, and Xinot's fury had melted away—but for small glowing embers still deep in her eyes, perhaps. It was not enough, anyway, to cause more problems. We spun and measured and *sliced*, smooth and clear and precise. We hummed some dreadful ditties, and we became ourselves and one another and the thread. I do not know what my sisters did on that day we did no work. We never spoke of it, and we did not ever speak of Monster again.

Eight

WE CLIMBED OUR ROCKY PATH SLOWLY, ONE BY one. It was slick from the rain, but we did not fear that. Serena went first, to pick out the way, then Xinot, and I came last, watching to catch my eldest sister in case she should stumble.

She didn't. She moved deliberately, choosing each step, but then hopped and climbed as fearlessly as Monster had used to do, using her cane as deftly as if it were a third leg. She lifted her face to the spray from time to time, and I thought I saw her smiling into it.

We were singing as we went. It was a journeying song, one to sing when your destination is unknown. It was jaunty, though it had a melancholy sort of twist. It weaved round the breeze and rolled with the surge. We were very soon wet.

Ours is not an easy island to reach; it took us much of the afternoon to cross the rocks, traveling at Xinot's pace. The final clouds were peeling back and the sky was showing its open face, a deep, glorious blue, by the time we'd come to the end and had climbed the tall sandy slope that hides us from the world. We shook out our hair; we wrung out our skirts. The sun would do the rest.

Xinot lifted her nose to the sparking breeze, and then she pointed into it, to the north and the west. Humans do not live on the land closest to our island. Shepherds graze their animals in the grasses there at times, but mostly it is empty, a wide stretch of rocky hills. In the direction that Xinot pointed, though, there had been several villages in our time.

Serena checked her bag of coins; I checked the ties on my packs. Xinot reached a hand into her left pocket, and something clattered there. I shot her a look. Her blades didn't sound like that.

But she was ignoring me; she sniffed again and started off ahead, leaving us hurrying to catch up.

It was like hearing a childhood tale again years after you have grown. The wind was warm, without the sting and freshness of the sea. The birds were loud, even deafening. I had forgotten how many birds there were, where there were so many leafy trees. Every sight was bright and soft. Every sound rang round and clear.

The smells, though, were the most overwhelming. Flowers— crocuses and heliotrope, lotuses and cherry blossoms—with such sweet and tangy scents as to set my mind abuzz. Green things were everywhere, and everywhere smelling of life and rain. We could even smell the dirt, dark and bitter, healthy, full.

The first time we came upon a shepherdess, walking toward us with her flock, we drew together and pulled the hoods of our dull gray cloaks down low. We did not want to frighten this girl, and we did not want to be recognized. We didn't know how you mortals would react to our presence after so many centuries apart.

But we needn't have worried. The girl called out a cheery "Good day" as she passed by. She smiled, and there was no smidge of anxiety in it. Three cloaked women headed toward the road—that's all we were to her. We didn't dare answer her back; we only nodded, but she saw nothing strange in that, either, and she and her flock were soon far away.

We looked at one another, surprised. We had not thought it would be that easy. When we had used to walk the human paths, we were always known. You would lower your eyes, knowing what dark mystery we took with us. You would speak if we spoke to you, not otherwise.

· But it happened again and again. Once we'd reached the road, we passed a farmer going to his fields, and another came by in a wagon, on his way to sell beets in a village square. They lifted their hats to us; they nodded. The one with the wagon offered Xinot a ride, and she could only blink while Serena assured him there was no need.

"Am I that ordinary, Chloe? Could you mistake me for

some weak mortal who needs a ride in a bumpy wagon?" Xinot asked when the man had gone.

I grinned at her. "Oh, grandmother, won't you take my arm? The road is rough for your old feet. Or maybe I should carry your things for you. You don't need such heavy burdens."

I reached out a hand toward her and was startled at how quickly she twisted, dropping her cane to hold her left pocket closed with both hands.

She shot me such a glare as would have withered that poor farmer where he sat. Even I backed away a step.

"I wouldn't dare," I said, and the teasing had gone from my voice. "You know that."

"Yes, don't be ridiculous, Xinot," Serena put in. "We're not going to look in your priceless pockets."

Xinot's scowl eased, and she picked up her cane. But I noticed she kept a few paces away from me after that.

We reached the first of the villages that evening, just as the stars were peeking out their heads. We had been following the scent of Aglaia's thread, and we could tell that she had passed through this village early this morning. We were far behind her, and we were moving slower, too; Xinot may not have needed a ride, but nor did she walk as quickly as a strong young girl.

When we stopped at a house marked as an inn at the edge of town, the man sitting in a chair out in the yard gave us a room readily enough, and once he was gone I shed my packs with relief.

I squinted through the cracks of our shuttered window out over a barley field.

"They've a fire going out there," I said. "A big one. I wonder if it's a festival day."

Serena slid in next to me. She popped the latch and pulled the shutter wide, leaning out into the breeze. "I don't know what it is," she said. "I'm going out to fetch some food. I'll ask the keeper what's going on."

As Xinot settled onto our hearth to watch the dust dance, I took up Serena's place and narrowed my eyes at the fire in the field. There was a dark figure at the front; if I concentrated, I could just see it waving its little arms and moving to and fro. And there were others standing and sitting in clumps all about the field near the fire. They were watching the figure, unmoving. They were as mesmerized by it as Xinot was by the corners of our fireplace.

"Someone's telling a story," I said when Serena came back with some bread and a slab of goat cheese.

"Yes," she said, discarding her cloak. "It's a storyteller, someone passing through. They have a tale most nights, though usually it's just a farmer or shopkeeper doing the telling. When I asked, the innkeeper looked as though he didn't know what to make of me, and I had to say we came from far away."

"Did you?" I said. "Did he suspect, do you think?"

"Oh, no," said Serena. She passed me a bit of cheese and I nearly forgot what we were talking about, the smell was so sharp, the taste was so crumbly and rich. "It's just that all the villages have storytelling after the sun goes down. It's a tradition in these parts, so he thought it strange that I needed to ask."

"*Cheese*," I said, then shook my head, focusing. "It's useful that they don't see us, anyway. They don't seem to have the slightest idea of what we are."

Xinot was toasting cheese and bread, balancing them on her stick over the coals. "They've forgotten," she said.

"Yes," said Serena. "I didn't think they would forget so soon."

I shook my head again, this time at them. "It isn't soon for mortals. For them, it is many spools of thread."

We ate in silence; the taste of such food soon overcame any thoughts we'd had of speaking. I convinced Xinot to melt some cheese for me, too, and when that gooey delight oozed into my mouth, I shut my eyes and didn't feel the darkness or see Aglaia's face or smell the salty spray of my far-off sea. I only chewed, and a very human sort of happiness slid down my throat, and I let it fill me.

Our days soon took up a new rhythm. That very next morning we rose early, paid our innkeeper, and set off down the road, smelling the wind, our backs to the rising sun. We walked at Xinot's pace all through the day, stopping now and again to rest beneath a shady tree or drink from a village well.

As we had the day before, we followed the scent of Aglaia's fate, and when the sun was setting, we found an inn for the night. We could not take out our glittering wool as we traveled, so we did our work in the dark of our rented room, where there were only the shadows in the hearth and the stars through the window to see. We dared not hum any songs, but we opened our shutters to let in the wind's whispers, and we fell softly into our art. And the next day we rose early again, paid our innkeeper, and set off down the road.

We soon understood the surprise of our first innkeeper at Serena asking about the storytelling. It was the end-of-day tradition in every town we passed—there was a traveling bard, or an ordinary villager who had learned to tell tales, in each one. Where there was a large enough inn, the towns-folk gathered in the evening to hear the stories, and where there wasn't, they came together in the village square or in a designated barn or out in a field somewhere.

It became our signal to stop for the night. When we came upon a group of you, drinking mugs of cider or mead, chil-dren falling asleep in laps, rapt faces focused on the night's teller, we would join you before we searched out food and a room. We were never turned away from a story.

Oh, we heard so many, those days that we followed Aglaia. Stories of gods and heroes, filled with forbidden love, brave acts, strange discoveries.

There were even tales of us; these mortals knew of our power and our thread. There were none, though, of the time when we had lived among you. In all these tales, we were separate, distant as the stars or thunder. We spun apart; we looked down into your lives from afar, tossing your threads over our shoulders into a heap when we were done.

There was truth in these tales. We hadn't paid attention to the human realm for ages; we couldn't. Still, the stories irri-tated me, for some foolish reason. I wanted to tell you about

Serena's children; when I saw a woman stroking a cat in her front yard, I wanted to stop and tell her about Monster, to set you right.

But you did not know us; you did not sense the power dripping from us, and I knew that it was better this way, in any case. We kept our hoods up; we drifted nameless through your lands.

And while it was thrilling to see your mortal world again, we all missed our rocks and our waves, and our nights at the edge of the sea. Sometimes, as the sky was beginning to lighten and we were packing away our tools for another long day, I thought of giving it up, of running back to our island, with my sisters or without them. I felt so heavy on these mornings. There was grittiness under my eyelids; my hair hung dull and limp. I rallied soon enough, as the sun murmured a greeting, as the birds started to sing. But I missed our wild home, and I knew my sisters did too.

Some nights, in fact, Xinot called an end to our work early. She rose from her chair or her seat on our bed; I heard that clattering in her pocket as she shuffled over to our door and out through the sleeping inn. Once, I started to follow her, but Serena held me back, whispering, "Let her go. She's been complaining to me of how crowded she feels here, of how there isn't any space to breathe. You know she's the least tied to the mortal realm; she needs more time with mysterious things."

So we let her go, and while Xinot wandered alone, Serena and I sat by our window, leaning out toward the stars. We didn't talk, but we listened to whatever echoes we could snatch of our magic; we watched for whatever tracings of our pattern might gleam.

It was only a few days into our journey when we started to hear stories of Aglaia from the people we met along the road— merchants traveling with their wares, a farmer's lass who gave us a drink of milk from her pail, some washerwomen we met as we cooled our feet in a stream. They'd seen her pass this way; even without us asking, many were eager to tell her tale.

Everyone had heard of her beauty, and of the raid on her village as well. We learned that after the raiders had gone, the neighboring villagers had come to put the bodies of Aglaia's family and friends to rest. They had been burned in a great fire out in the nearby fields; no one had picked through the remains to tally every person.

That she lived seemed a wonder to these people.

"Poor little thing," we heard from our innkeeper one evening; he had given her a room the night before. "All alone in the world!"

"Not alone," his daughter replied. "Didn't you hear? She won't be alone for long."

"Hush," the man said. "That's only a rumor; we don't know for certain yet."

After we'd gone to our room, Serena wondered aloud if the girl might have heard some news of Aglaia's pregnancy. I only shrugged, but I had a different idea, and that very next day we started to hear another name entwined with hers.

Endymion.

I hadn't told my sisters about him, but Endymion was a hero to his people; soon enough we knew all the tales. We learned how he had fought a dragon and pierced its flaming heart. How he had led his soldiers into battle, again and again, helmetless so that his locks flew back in the wind and his war cry echoed against the sky—how he inspired such fear in his enemies and such loyalty in his men, numbers of soldiers did not matter, only courage, only bloodlust. How he had sailed across the sea and come back with a gleaming crown set with jewels never seen and the head of a giant whose eyes opened wider than cart wheels.

He was a myth already, and he was still a young man.

The people we met were sure that Aglaia was headed toward Endymion's city. He ruled them from there; he was prince over all the land we traveled through. And he was loved. The people's faces glowed when they talked of him. He had brought peace and prosperity to his land.

We had been told, the second night of our travels, that it would be a six days' journey to Endymion's city; as we grew closer, it seemed that the rumors of Aglaia and this prince became more precise by the hour—and more joyful.

"She has come to marry him," a miller's wife told us as she passed with a wagon filled with bags of flour. "She was glowing with her gladness."

A wheelwright standing in the sun outside his shop confirmed it. "There is to be a wedding. He thought her dead. We all did."

"Was he happy to know that she lived?" Serena asked. I could not stand the hope in her voice.

"Happy?" The wheelwright turned an unbelieving face toward her. "It is the best thing in his life."

He loves her, they said. *She loves him*. Again and again, everywhere we went. The hero was to marry his love; the beauty was to marry her prince. The whole land was to celebrate.

"It is too bad," I said once to a girl who was walking her geese alongside us, "that the lady's family is not alive to see her married."

"Oh," she said, "but it is a miracle that she survived. That is what she says. A miracle that she lives to be wed."

So, not a whiff of grief was to darken Aglaia's wedding. Not a hint of trouble to worry her bridegroom—who was also the father of her child, I was certain. This prince was not used to refusal.

I could see the moment my sisters began to believe in Endymion's glory. I saw how they walked with lighter steps, how they breathed freer and smiled at the people we met. They thought the girl was on her way to destiny. Not one that shrieked and shattered, but something full and beautiful, the nicest sort of end.

I let them believe it; I had to, didn't I? I couldn't expose them to the twistedness, the rot I had smelled on Endymion's thread. I had to keep it from them for as long as I could and hope that Aglaia's future would be happier than her past, that this journey would end with us seeing the girl settled into as contented a life as my sisters dreamed.

It was all I could do: stay silent as we heard the stories of this brave young prince and the things they were saying about Aglaia—*Lucky girl. He always loved her. Now she'll have a chance to be happy!*—and pray that my sisters wouldn't notice the darker underbelly hidden on the flip side of these green leaves.

Nine

A DAY BEFORE WE WERE TO REACH THE CITY, THE scent of Aglaia's thread veered off to the east. We stood at the crossroads, smelling it. We knew the way to Endymion lay straight ahead. When a woman came by with a basket of freshly picked flowers, we asked where Aglaia's road would lead us, if we were to take it.

"Oh, that," she said. "Just a few villages, some fields. If you're looking for the city, it's on ahead." She pointed in the direction we had been heading.

"Nothing else?" I said. "Only fields and villages?"

"Well . . ." She thought, and then she said, "I suppose, a good day's walking, there's also that sad ruin. The village where our Aglaia used to live, the one who's to marry our prince. Nothing's left of that, though. There's no reason to visit."

We thanked her, and we let her go her way, and then we turned east.

That night I asked our innkeeper a few pointed questions when I went down from our room to fetch some food. Yes, Aglaia had passed through here only the day before. Yes, her old village lay to the east; we'd reach it late tomorrow morning if we set out early enough.

Yes, he could tell me where the oracle lived who had given the children of that town their prophecies. She was the same oracle he had asked prophecies of for his own children. His round face brightened, and he began to tell me what those were, how they had been promised contented lives, luck, lots of love.

I cut him off; I think he was offended. But I could not stand his naïveté, and after I'd grabbed some bowls of soup, I turned from him and walked away.

I did not tell my sisters that next day where I was going; I left them as soon as we were out of town. I said there was a place I had heard of, with views to the north and the east. I said that maybe I could catch a glimpse of the sea, or maybe Endymion's city.

Serena offered to come along with me; I shrugged her off.

"The path would be steep for Xinot," I said, and when my eldest sister snorted, I went on, "Oh, leave me alone, will you? If *she* can run outside in the middle of the night and we aren't allowed to follow, I think you can let me climb one hill all by myself!"

Xinot said, "What's this about not being allowed to follow?"

"Oh," said Serena, "I told her what you said about feeling penned in by all these people."

"Penned in!" said Xinot. "I never said that. I sound like a sheep."

"Yes, you did. You know you did." Serena was beginning to look harried, and I grabbed the moment.

"If Xinot can feel penned in, then so can I!" I said, and started up a nearby hill.

"Of course you can," said Serena, hardly paying me attention now. "You can catch us up along the road. Go safe!" And she turned again to smoothing Xinot's ruffled feathers.

It wasn't far. A few hills, around several copses of trees. No crop fields grew near her cave; it was a wild area, with brush and bushes and rocky streams. There was a large, flat stone in the valley just to the south of her place; it was scattered with brass coins and some wilted blue flowers.

I paused before it. I thought of sweeping them off, these meager offerings. But then I pulled my cloak tighter around me to hide my anger, and I climbed the final slope to the entrance of her cave.

"Who goes there?" The voice came almost at once, drifting on a chill breeze down the winding passageway.

I stepped in toward it. One turn, two, and the cave opened out into a large round chamber. I'd no need to blink away the sun; I saw in the dark as well as any owl or lion, and still I could not see all the corners of this room.

She sat in a sort of chair made of cave rock in the center, her hands placed flat along its rough arms, her feet flat against the earth. Her hair was long, and it hung down free over her shoulders as mine usually does. She must have rushed over to this seat as she heard me entering and positioned herself where she'd seem the most akin to our magic.

"Who are you?" she said. "What do you seek?"

Now I saw how a clever jutting of rock hid another tunnel, off to the left. She'd have an actual home in there, with a bed and a place to cook. If the offerings out in the valley were any indication, she lived much better than most dwellers of caves.

I didn't come any closer than the end of the entrance tunnel. It was cold here; I didn't mind that. It reminded me of the wintry days on our island, when the wind scratched and bit. I breathed in this misty place, and I felt my fury at this woman growing.

"There was a girl," I said, as calmly as I could manage.

The oracle tilted her head at me, and I hated its haughtiness. "There are many girls."

"You gave her a prophecy."

"As I do."

"Not like this one. You gave her three words. The first was *beauty*. The second was *clarity*."

I stopped, and she said, "Beauty, clarity—a good fortune." There was no uncertainty in her voice. There was no fear of me, or of what she had done, or of the power she had played with so cavalierly.

If I had wondered before, I knew now. Any true oracle would have known me on sight.

"Not the last word," I said. "It was something that made her parents look at each other with fear."

There was silence in the cave. "What does it matter to you?"

"It matters," I said. "I will not go until you tell me that third word."

"Will you not?" She stood; she came a few steps closer, and she squinted at me. I looked back at her, not straining at all to see the gray hairs on her head, the slight limp as she walked.

After a long moment, she turned, and she went back to her chair again. She sat tall in it, and her dark dress melted into the stone and earth and cold.

"I will tell you," she said, and she was offhand, looking somewhere over my head. "There is no reason not to. The girl isn't around to object."

She hadn't heard the rumors, then. Out in her cave, she'd be the one person in the land, maybe, who didn't know that Aglaia had lived through the raid, that she was on her way to destiny.

She said, "You are right. I gave the child three words. The first was *beauty*. The second was *clarity*."

She paused so long that I said, with something of a snarl, "The third word, oracle."

She did not want to say it, but she did. "The third word, stranger, that I gave the girl was *pain*."

Pain. *Pain.* Aglaia's final word, the thing that shaped her life—not just today, not just tomorrow, but the whole bright thread of the girl's long life. Beauty, clarity, and *pain*.

I did not want to believe it. I would not believe it.

Was this how it felt to be a mortal, bound to a path and unable to change it? Was this the same ridiculous refusal of acceptance that drove men and women to our doorstep, begging us to spin them a new thread? I had thought such mortals sad and insolent and slightly crazed. But my refusal was not sadness or insanity. I was simply making a clear and knowledgeable choice that the world must not be the way it was.

Who was this woman, anyway, to say this was how the world was?

"Why would you give a child a prophecy like that?" I was almost hissing, it was so low. "What could possess you?"

The oracle drew upright, her hands against her knees. "I am only the voice," she said, sure and proud. Her eyes were deep as the corners of her cave. "I listen to the darkness, and I feel it moving through me. I could no more alter its meaning than I could change my own fate. I am the instrument, and it is the hand that sweeps along my strings."

I laughed, though there was no joy in it, and the oracle glanced at me with surprise, straight into my face. I turned from her. I steadied my breathing; I pulled my hood lower, forcing the power to drip out of my voice back into the dark. I said, "Except for this one girl, you give the children of these villages each the same prediction, though they could not possibly all live long and happy lives."

"Not all," said the oracle. She was angry, but there was a brush now of wariness to her. I should not have laughed.

"Some are given long and happy lives, as you say," she went on. "Others are not so lucky. I do not conceal the darker fates."

I said, impatient, "You add enough variation that the villagers keep coming back. If you gave them all exactly the same words, they would not look to you for their prophecies, for they could not pretend then that you were not a fraud."

"I am not a fraud!"

"How much do they pay you for your services? Do you give the better fates to the ones with the larger money bags?"

She stood, her chin high and her eyes flashing, and she thought that she could intimidate me. I should have stepped back from her; I should have cowered. My anger was rising again, though. This woman made a game of forces she could not understand. She earned a living by the worst sort of falsehood—she demeaned the glory of our threads.

I said, only just managing to keep from throwing back my hood, letting my hair fall loose and my voice shine dark, "It is a dangerous game you play. There are those who might object to it, those who have the means to make their objections known."

She wanted to throw me from her cave. She wanted to call down some toothless curses on me, some little rhymes that would have scared her villagers half to death. She was as in love with the power as I was—only mine was real.

Something held her back, though. I wasn't ordinary enough, even with my old gray cloak. There was an edge to me she hadn't encountered before.

She said, still angry but keeping herself in check, "Who are you? I've never seen you in these parts."

I almost laughed again. Who did she think I was? Surely not the youngest of my sisters. Perhaps a rich lady or a princess even, come to seek a fortune but wanting to be sure she was legitimate? That would explain why she had given me the word so easily. I drew back, toward the tunnel. "It doesn't make any difference who I am."

But she was following me now, trying to peer beneath my hood. I turned my face away.

"If you mean to stir up trouble for me, it won't work. I've been giving out prophecies for many years, longer than most of my villagers can remember. They won't believe you if you speak against me, no matter who you are."

"I didn't come to stir up trouble."

"No? Why did you come, then?"

Now I was sidling farther away, down the tunnel to the entrance. The woman was right. There was no point in staying longer. She had given me the word I wanted; there wasn't anything to be gained by scolding her.

The light would be behind me now, casting my face in deeper shadow. Still she was trying to see me clear, matching me step for step.

"I have what I came for," I told her. "I will leave you in peace."

"What?" said the oracle. "You came to heckle me? Or . . . no." She had stopped, and I stopped too, halted by the sudden understanding in her voice. "You came because of that girl.

Aglaia. You're about the same age, too. But you're not her. You can't be. She died in the raid, along with everyone she knew."

Pain. "Did she?" I said, too quiet, too deadly. "If that were true, how would your prophecy be fulfilled? Beauty, yes; she had always been beautiful. And clear sight—no doubt she had that, too. But where, oracle, was the third word? Where in the shape of that girl's village life was the *pain?*"

The oracle had frozen. I scarcely cared. My rage was trickling all through me now, familiar and strong. I let my eyes spark. I let my hood fall back enough that my hair swept out along my cheeks, black and gleaming.

She said, hardly a breath, "You . . ."

It was not possible that she recognized me. Not this charlatan, with her false promises and falser pride. She would not know her own fate if it tapped her on the shoulder.

Somehow, though, I had gotten her wrong. She did know me. As she stood there, breathless, bracing herself against the tunnel wall, there was the same awe in her face as had been in the mortals who had known us all those centuries ago.

I pulled my hood down low again. I backed away from her.

"Mistress," she said, reaching a hand in my direction. "Please. Wait."

I paused, not speaking, not moving toward her.

She stood straight again. She was not lacking in courage, then. Only integrity. "I was not lying about the girl's prophecy," she said.

I waited, huddled in my cloak.

"It is true that most of my predictions are not . . . specifically tailored for each baby. I always ask the darkness for the child's future, but hardly ever am I given an answer. Sometimes, though. I am not the fraud you think; I have heard the voice of your power murmuring in my cave. First, when I was a little girl, it told me this was to be my path, that I was to dedicate myself to it. And then, on and off again, throughout the years. They are not usually joyful predictions, the ones given to me to share. At least when I do shape my own, they are reassuring, or touchstones through difficulties.

"I would not . . . I never would give a child a prophecy of pain. Not unless I had no choice. Not unless the mystery I serve demanded it of me."

She was silent then. I didn't want to believe her. It would have been easy to walk away, dismissing her words as just another lie.

As she spoke, though, I had felt the darkness in the room beyond swirling, thickening. I knew its scent. I should have known it the moment I entered the cave. I should have recognized this brush along my cheek, the way its power flowing through my lungs gave me such energy, made me face down this woman with such fury. I didn't understand it. What could have kept me from knowing the touch of my own magic?

The oracle said, "If you tell me to leave my work and never return, I will. Only know, mistress, that I have never betrayed a true prophecy, and I have never sought to use my position to harm anyone."

I closed my eyes against her. For whatever reason, the darkness loved this one. It was creeping along her arms, burrowing into her hair. "No," I said, and I didn't bother to take the edge from my voice anymore. "I would not ask that of you. I haven't . . . I haven't the right, in any case, to take you from your path."

She let out her breath, soft.

"Thank you," I said, though the words tasted sour. "For your help."

She nodded, and then I did turn away. I left her behind with her terrible truths, throwing myself to the warm summer arms of the sun.

It wasn't a fake prophecy; it was a true one. It hadn't been this woman's fault, but the fault of our own darkness, and the path we had given Aglaia was even more horrible than I had imagined.

I did not let myself think as I rushed from the cave, as I hurried back to the road where I had left my sisters and then on, to the east, across hill after hill. I wanted only to be with them again. I wanted only to take out my wool and my spindle, to sit with them beneath some tree, to forget the third word, the oracle's truth, the bright, burning eyes of Aglaia. I wanted only to shed this knowledge as a dripping cloak, to diminish into the Chloe that I knew, untroubled, the surest of us.

I did not think, so I did not realize I had reached it until I was stepping past the leaning walls of her village, down her streets. Then I saw, and I stopped, and I dropped my bags and stood there. There wasn't a spell my sister could have cast to take away this pain.

There was not even a word for what was left of Aglaia's village.

Ruin. Desolation. Tragedy.

They are thin, insufficient things, words. They conjure abstractions, not actualities. They speak in the present, not of the past that drifted like a song through the tumbled stones and scattered pieces of this world—the grubby shirt left spread across a stump, maybe to dry; the bucket lying beside a well, grass inching up and around; the earthen bowls still stacked high, now displayed for the world to see, their cupboard door clinging to a lone hinge.

It hadn't been long enough for this place not to feel as though its inhabitants might come back any day. They might come walking up that path through the overgrown pear and fig orchards, chattering, and fall silent one by one as they saw the dirtiness, the brokenness awaiting them. *So much work*, they would say to one another. *It will take so long to set this to rights.*

See, but they would do it; they would set it to rights, building new walls and attaching cupboards, shaking out that shirt with a grimace and filling that bucket with fresh, clean water. It would be work, but they would do it. This village was waiting for them; any day now, they might arrive.

My sisters stood in the center of the village, where the paths met, where there might have been stories in the evening and the children would have gathered to play their games. They were not speaking; they did not acknowledge me as I came up next to them, dragging my packs, dragging my feet as well.

Of course we had heard of this before, of entire villages disappearing, their every citizen dead, gone, all *snapping* off at once.

It was different not only because we were here, but because we saw it through her eyes. It was different because it belonged to her.

"She will find whoever did this," Serena said, and I had never heard her voice so sure and heated. "She will find them, and she will kill them."

"Yes," said Xinot. "Of course she will."

Endymion. I could not say a thing.

We stood, for hours it seemed, unable to move or stop staring. "What did you see from your hill, Chloe?" Serena asked after several eternities. "Could you catch a glimpse of our sea?"

I opened my mouth to lie to her, then closed it again. She was already crying, though she smiled at me through the tears. Surely there could be no protecting her, not after she had seen this. It was too horrible, too broken, too *real*. She and Xinot would know the third word even if I never told them. They would understand the thing that shaped Aglaia's path.

"We must keep on," I said at last. "She will be far ahead of us now. I will tell you everything along the way."

Ten

ENDYMION.

This was his city. This, with its white stone walls gleaming in the sun, with its yellow streets and colorful market squares. Leafy trees lined the wider avenues; ripe figs hung above the heads of passersby, so that you had only to reach to grab at sweetness.

There were poor, but their rags seemed cleaner and their faces rounder. There were rich, but more of them stopped to share their coin, and more of them took time to smile up into the sky, watching the wispy white clouds dancing by.

We could not deny that the prince of such a city was a hero. Endymion was no fake, no bloated pig or sniveling weakling. When Endymion went to war, he won. When he put his mind to solving some problem in his city, it was solved. When he wooed a beautiful girl . . . well, she came back to him in the end, didn't she? With steps of joy and purpose, thrilling over her fate. Leaving a trail of celebration in her wake, like crumbs of cake.

Here the air shimmered with stories of Aglaia.

She arrived just yesterday!

Is she as lovely as they say?

A fervent nod. *More. I hear the gods themselves are jealous of her.*

That one made us look at one another worriedly. No mortal wants the gods becoming jealous, especially of a thing like beauty. The most beautiful gods are not known for their intelligence, or for their kindness.

"Our prince," we heard one little beggar child say, her curls surprisingly pretty, "will marry her this very week!"

He loves her.

She loves him.

The bards will tell their story through the ages.

It was agreed upon and rejoiced at; it seemed that everyone was coming out into the streets, giving up their work, and talking it over from every angle.

It was the easiest thing to find out where she was staying. She had arrived early yesterday afternoon, so we had managed to make up time in our last frantic rush back from her village and north to Endymion's city. It was said that the prince would come down out of his grand house to pay her a call this evening, to declare his everlasting devotion and to bring her back with him.

In the meantime, she had taken a room at an inn in a

modest section of the city, for which humbleness she was much praised.

"And she to be our princess!" a clothier said.

The wine seller next to him clapped his shoulder. "A girl of the people. She'll not forget where she came from."

My sisters had not wanted to hear me when I told them that the raiders who had destroyed Aglaia's village had not been raiders at all, but the man it seemed she was giving herself to, and his loyal soldiers. I showed them his thread; I made them smell the rotting at its core. They had not wanted to hear the prophecy, either, but they had listened, and they hadn't questioned its truth. Last night, our final night on the road, Xinot had disappeared for hours, and when she came back, she clattered the thing in her pocket so unceasingly that when she stopped, my mind still shook with its echo.

"You should have told us long ago," Serena had said as we started out this morning.

"Nonsense," said Xinot. "She was protecting you from it."

"And you," I couldn't help saying, though my eldest sister glared. "I am the strongest-willed of us, Xinot."

"Oh, yes," she said, "your strong will has kept us so safe from this girl's pain."

I snapped, "I never would have told you if we hadn't seen her village."

Serena said, "But you didn't try to keep us from that, Chloe."

I stared at her; she was right. I could have argued against taking that path. I could have said we should go on ahead and make it to the city before Aglaia backtracked.

I said, much softer, "I didn't think of it."

Xinot said, "Or didn't want to. You were determined to seek out that oracle, after all, and what good could that have done?"

"I was angry," I said. "I thought she was false."

"There are hundreds of false oracles," said Xinot. "Why did you care about this one so particularly?"

Serena laid a hand on our sister's arm. "She cares about the girl," she said. "Of course she wanted to know the third word."

And I wanted to say no, that I didn't care, not as she had about her children, not as they had about our cat. Not in a way that could turn me from our calling, not ever.

But I must have been fated not to respond, because just at that moment, something was stuck in my throat. I swallowed, and my eyes teared up with it. Serena reached across to tuck my hair back gently, and I didn't shake her off.

As we slipped through the streets of Endymion's city, we drew no wondering looks. All were busy gossiping and laughing; all were immersed in Aglaia's happy ending. A crowd had gathered outside her inn, and a woman pointed out her window willingly. We went around to the back of the building and came in through the kitchen.

We have come to visit Aglaia, we told the lad there as he looked up from his chopping.

He gestured behind us toward the door with his knife. "You and everyone else," he said. "Get away with you."

We drew back our hoods. *Not us and everyone else,* we said. *Just us.*

Well. It was nice to know that mortals kept a place for us, after all, that your forgetting was as Aglaia's spell had been, out on our island: throw away the veil, confront you with the truth, and you could see again with clear, if frightened eyes.

He was not capable of speaking after that. Xinot led the way past him through the kitchen, Serena following close behind. As I walked by the lad, I ran one finger along his cheek and smiled a very small smile. I felt his eyes watching me all the rest of the way.

We paused outside the door to her room.

We could hear her singing. Just a small tune, a hum of violets dripping with rain, of rich dark soil, ready for tilling. It was a song she would have learned as a child, growing up on the slopes and in the valleys of her land, watching her family plant their vines and prune their fruit trees. It was a song from the middle of life, where there are no wonderings of where you are to find your purpose and where there are no worries about what's coming at the end. Where the rhythm of the days is sacred, because each waking and each sunset is fulfillment—you have done it, you have found the way to happiness in life. Family, hard work, stories around the fire: one such day, you think, would be reason enough for a life.

There was no hidden wrongness in this song; I had no wish to push Aglaia from a boat to make her stop. As I listened, I thought that I had heard the tune before, but I could not think where.

When I turned to ask Serena, there were tears in her eyes.

"What's wrong?" I murmured.

She shook her head. "The most beautiful things," she said, and stopped.

"What?"

"It is always a miracle, that there are beautiful things."

"Is it?" It seemed to me that the world was filled with beautiful things, that you could no more take away the violets or the stories than you could Xinot's *snap* at the end.

Serena only smiled, through the tears. "I would say you'd understand when you are older . . ."

I laughed softly. "I am as old as you, sister."

"In years," said Serena.

"Is that not how we determine age?"

"Chloe," Xinot said suddenly, and we both looked at her. "Stop being stupid."

I opened my mouth, ready with a retort, but she held up two curled fingers. Aglaia's song had stopped. We opened the door, and she was looking at us.

She was sitting alone on her bed. She watched as we filed in, as we closed her door again and stood in a semicircle before it.

This room must have been the grandest in the inn. A merchant or a minor landowner might have stayed here with his spouse in that good-size bed. The fireplace was clean and big; the window was shuttered with pretty painted wood.

I don't think Aglaia was seeing any of it. Her hair was tidy; her tunic was smoothed. She sat with exact posture at the end of the mattress, her hands tucked between her knees. She was not gone, as she had been when Serena's spell was in full force. Her eyes sparked and her mouth quirked sardonically to see us again. But she was in thrall to another sort of spell: a path, a purpose.

"You," said Aglaia at last.

Us, we said.

"Have you been following me all this way?"

Yes, we said.

"Why? What do you want?"

Serena said, gently, "What are you going to do?"

"What do you think?" said Aglaia. "I am going to kill him."

We nodded. It was reasonable.

"And the child?" said Serena.

Aglaia smiled, and again I was surprised at how much life there was behind it. The world to this girl would seem pale and thin. We three must seem little more than clinging mists or floating phantoms. "My child will be rich," said Aglaia, "and powerful, and happy. My child will have its birthright, everything it should."

We nodded again. We did not disbelieve her.

Again she said, "What do you want? Is there something that you can do for me?"

I turned my face from her; I did not want to answer. She had asked for my help so many times, and so many times I had refused her.

Serena said, "Probably there is nothing we can do."

Aglaia looked back and forth between us. "Can you kill him for me?"

We shook our heads. *We're not allowed to do that.*

"Can you tell me whether or not I will succeed?"

No. We cannot tell you what the thread has said.

Aglaia let out her breath, looking over at the window, through which the sun was eavesdropping. We could hear the murmuring of the crowd below, each hoping to catch a glimpse of their prince's wife-to-be. "What good are you, then?"

Not much, we admitted.

Then Xinot tapped her fingers against her cane and said, sharp and excited, "We could toss the bones."

We looked at her.

"It's not as dependable as reading the thread," said Xinot. "It's only a fortune-telling trick, but we are better at it than most."

"I'm sure you are," said Aglaia. She narrowed her eyes, considering. "But I've no bones."

"Oh, I have," said Xinot. She reached into her left-hand pocket, where she kept her shears, where she kept that clattering, clattering thing. Aglaia watched warily. Out came Xinot's fingers, laced with the spine and ribs of a fish and dripping with many tinier bones.

I leaned over them. "Have you been carrying these all this while?"

Serena said, "Is this where you go in the middle of the night? To play with your toys?"

All those times I'd thought my sister too otherworldly to bear the press of the mortal realm, all those times I'd watched her slip from our room and felt an awe at the mystery that measured the length of her veins. "*Xinot,*" I hissed, and couldn't say anything more.

She said, placid enough to enrage, "I get bored."

Then Aglaia was moving over toward the fireplace and sitting down upon the floor. We followed her; we sat in a circle, the four of us, and of course it reminded me of the many nights we had sat like this, facing one another across our fire pit as a fish smoked deliciously on the grill.

Aglaia saw me watching her. "What is it?" she said, though without any friendliness.

"Do you remember?" I said. "Do you remember it at all?"

Serena poked me. "Hush," she said, and Aglaia hadn't opened her mouth to answer. I didn't want her to look the way she did—angry, as if the only thing keeping her from snarling at us was the hope that our fish-bone predictions might help.

Some hope. We might be better at it than most fortune-tellers, but tossing the bones is a notoriously unreliable way of seeing the future. Fish bones do not tell the truth, not in the way that our threads do. They tell stories, when they aren't spouting nonsense, and most fortune-tellers could not separate the fiction from its fragile strand of prophecy.

Still, as we weren't allowed to read Aglaia's thread for her, this was the next best thing. Xinot flicked her wrist, and the bleached bits tumbled across the wood floor between us.

They scattered, a little one landing a finger's width from Serena's heel, a rib bone pointing its ridge toward Aglaia's right eye.

I bent forward, my hair across my face. Serena clasped her hands on her knees, and Xinot crouched as crookedly as ever, her cane laid behind her, a small smile twitching.

"Well?" Aglaia said, and we all three hushed her.

A swimming bird, Xinot said.

A flying fish, said Serena.

I scrunched my eyes; the bones wavered in the dim sunlight, between my strands of hair. The shadows crept, and crept; a murky finger traced along my cheekbone.

I felt a horror.

I said, *Something has gone devastatingly wrong.*

A burning sea, Xinot said.

A frozen fire, said Serena.

I said, *There is an end to patterns. All the threads are coming loose.*

The bones rattled on the floor, though no one touched them. The room flashed dark, and my eyes and the eyes of my sisters rolled back in our heads. We said, as one, *We will be to blame.*

Then it was gone.

I was breathing fast, hard. My neck was slick with sweat. We looked about at one another. I held Xinot's gaze, and she shook her head. "Not now," she said. "Not for a while yet."

"It might not happen," Serena said.

Xinot's fingers flicked. "It might not."

Aglaia said, "What did that mean?"

"A good question," I said. "Any ideas?"

But Xinot was still shaking her head. She reached out to gather her bones, and she dropped them back into her pocket;

I heard that clattering as they settled against her shears. "I have been casting these bones over and over again. Always they tell me a similar tale, of impossible things, of catastrophe. I don't know what it means."

"They're only fish bones," I said. "You cannot trust them."

She looked at me, without a smile. "Chloe, you felt what I felt. Are you going to tell me it was not true?"

I looked away.

Serena said again, softly, "It might not happen. Prophecies do not always come true."

"It might not," Xinot repeated, but not as though she believed it.

Aglaia was frowning, watching us. "It has nothing to do with me or my baby, though?"

Xinot said, "We don't know. It might."

Aglaia said, "But you haven't any idea what it would mean for us?"

"No."

Aglaia pushed to her feet, stepping out of our circle. She turned her back on us; she went over to the window and poked one finger through the shutters to peek at the crowd in the street. "They love me," she said.

We were silent.

"They came out to see me, all along the road. They wanted to touch my hand; they wanted to tell me how happy they were that I had survived after all. They wanted to wish me joy." Her hand fell back to her side and the shutters closed, but she did not turn from them. "Joy," she said.

I wrapped my arms around my knees; I held my face against my skirt. There had been no *joy* in the oracle's fortune.

"Why did you follow me?" Aglaia asked us again.

Now Serena tried to answer. "Yours is a powerful path, Aglaia. We are drawn to such paths; we wanted to see it to its end."

I shook my head against my skirt, but I doubt any of them saw. She was right. I knew that she was right about Aglaia's path, about us being drawn. There was something missing, though, and my throat was caught again, with that thing that made it impossible to speak.

I wouldn't have known what I wanted to say anyway.

In the silence, we could hear the murmur of the crowd rising excitedly. I lifted my head. Aglaia was peeking through the shutters again. Xinot had moved to a chair near the empty fireplace; she was staring into its depths. Serena had her face turned up toward the girl.

A clattering, not like Xinot's bones—harsher, louder. Many horses, coming toward the inn. I got to my feet and went over next to Aglaia. She twisted her summer-sea eyes toward me and moved over to make room. We peered out through the shutters together.

The crowd was moving to either side of the street. At first we couldn't see anything arriving; we only heard the clattering getting harsher, getting louder, and then they came stomping in, a whole troop of them. Horses with gleaming flanks, soldiers in glinting armor and colorful tunics. At the front was an unarmored man on a golden stallion, leading a pretty white mare. His hair was as bright as his horse's mane. He sat tall and smiled about at the crowd with flashing teeth.

I knew who this was; I knew what lay behind that golden smile, and I hated him. My hair was beginning to drift, sliding through the shutters as though it would have liked to reach out and strangle him where he sat. It had that power, you know. If I'd been allowed to take lives, I could have set him on fire with one word and then watched as he burned away to ash.

Next to me, Aglaia's breathing had changed. The shutters were rattling, only just a bit as she trembled. Then something hardened in her face, and they stopped.

I said, watching her, "You don't have to go with him. No one will make you."

She said, "Yes, Chloe, I do," and for a moment it was as though we were back in the boat, the way she said my name, the way there wasn't any anger in her voice.

If she hadn't said it in that way, I wouldn't have offered. "I could go with you."

She looked at me, and for an instant I thought she might say yes. Then she backed away from the window, and from me. She dropped her hand to her side; she smoothed her skirt. She stood straight, and determined, and as tall as that man. Even in this dim room, her loveliness stunned. Xinot turned from the fireplace; Serena got to her feet.

We all watched as Aglaia pulled her head up high, as she said, without any trace now of familiarity, "No, you mustn't follow me. There isn't any way for you to help. We've determined

that. I must go alone and do it myself. It's my path, after all."
And, flat, with maybe a slight bitter twist, "My destiny."

She took a breath; it filled her up and set her toward the door. She left us there to go down through the inn and out into the street, where Endymion and all his people were waiting.

Eleven

WE WATCHED THAT FIRST MEETING FROM THE window, silent shadows in a row, peering through the shutters.

The crowd quieted as the girl came out of the inn. She stopped at the bottom of the steps; she made a bow to Endymion. He smiled at her. It was a beautiful smile, and there was no fear in it. He didn't know that she knew. For him, this was the ending he had always believed he deserved.

As Aglaia walked up next to him, she smiled back, and it was as beautiful as his. He said something to her; she laughed, and if I hadn't seen her trembling beside me at this window only minutes earlier, I might have believed it too. There were answering smiles all through the crowd. Some of the women were holding their hands to their mouths or chests, tearing up.

He offered her the pretty white mare. One of his men

dismounted to help her climb up; she took his hand but kept her eyes always on the prince. When she had settled onto the mare's back, Endymion leaned close to her, and closer, and then, there in front of all his people, he was kissing her, and she did not flinch or wrinkle her nose or claw out his eyes. I don't know how, but she kissed him back and smiled again when he leaned away.

They turned and rode up the street together, and the crowd strewed flowers all along their way.

Some time after they had gone, an old woman, back bent, hunched over her cane, came up to our room and walked in on us without knocking.

Our cloaks were still puddled on the floor before the fireplace. We hadn't yet managed to leave the window, to turn away from where the girl had gone. The daylight was fading and lamps were being lit; we could still hear the stir of happy gossip in the crowd, which was only now beginning to disperse.

We looked toward the woman, and she crinkled her face at us. She said, "You gave my boy a fright."

We blinked, remembering. The boy in the kitchen, the one who had tried to stop us from coming into the inn.

Serena said, calm and sweet, "Please accept our apologies—"

"Don't worry yourself, mother," the woman said.

My sister lost the rest of her words.

"The lad will live. He's seen stranger things in my inn."

I peered at the woman, sniffing for traces of the scent that had clung to the oracle's cave, the scent I hadn't taken the time to search for until I'd made a fool of myself. There was nothing, only dry old skin and soap.

She pointed her nose at me. "Checking me over, maidy? I'm not a ghost or a ghoulie, just an old mortal with eyes to see." She opened them wide at me, and they were filmy, their lights already fading.

Xinot said, "Innkeeper, we will be needing a room."

The woman said, "Have you coin?"

"Of course," said Xinot.

She shrugged. "Then have this one, if you like. How long will you be staying?"

"You needn't fear," said Xinot. "We bring no troubles for you."

There was a silence. The woman chuckled. "You think that I am feared of you, crone?"

Serena murmured, "Most people are."

"I am not feared of powerless things."

The silence now was thick. Aglaia's last glance, the one when she had almost let me come with her, flashed before me. She had gone down to him alone; she had kissed him. She was with him now, and I hadn't strangled him, and I hadn't burned him to bits.

I said, *Watch yourself, old one.*

"Oh, you don't like that," the woman said. "You've been dabbling in little truths for ages; I would think you'd be immune to the things."

Little truths? I said. *Dabbling?*

"Chloe," said Serena.

"Who's the mistress here?" the woman said. "Yours are the spinning fingers, maidy, but who shears you the wool?"

Serena was holding me back now from crossing the room to this upstart. If she thought her age would grant her leniency, she was in for a rude surprise. I cared not how many summers she had seen. I'd been around before the seasons started.

My *spinning fingers* were itching for a spell, one not nearly as mild as Serena's memory trick. "Let me go," I spat.

She whispered back, "Chloe, she doesn't know what she is saying."

The old woman was watching us patiently, leaning onto her cane. "Oh, I don't doubt that you have to power to kill me, little girl. With the tip of one fingernail, I'm sure. With one scratch on my withered face.

"Tell me this, though. You came to see that girl, the one Endymion is going to marry. You talked with her; you sat with her before the fire." She gestured at our discarded cloaks. "Then she went away, and you didn't follow. Maybe, whatever your task here is, it's finished. So why did you ask me for a room?"

Xinot said, "That is nothing to do with you."

The woman shrugged again. "No, but I'm old, and I don't mind being bothersome. The city is beside itself with joy, you know. Our prince, his destined bride." Her eyebrows went up. "Isn't she?"

Serena's hand was slackening on my arm, but I was frozen where I stood. This woman, without even a name, without beauty or clear sight—she was all I could see, all I could hear.

"She didn't say much to me," the woman went on. "I doubt she says much to anyone. She smiled, but I know the difference between a smile and happiness. I couldn't see it very well, the way she must have held her head up high, the excited flutter of her fingers as she talked with me and my boy of our prince. But I could hear the way she labored for breath in between her words. I could feel the hitch at the ends of her sentences, so slight, just a nervous habit maybe, except what does she have to be nervous about? Not our destined princess, not as she goes to meet her fate."

"You think we are blind to this?" Serena said.

"I think," said the woman, "that you have not walked the mortal realm in many ages, and that there is a reason for that. I think the stories they tell of you are true—that you do your work without a care for its result, that you, who should be the wisest of creatures, don't even understand your own art."

I said, finally, snarling at her, shaking off my sister's arm completely but staying at her side, "Mortal, you are overfull of your few years. You talk to us of understanding—us, who have seen the birth of stars. Us, who measured your life before you knew you existed; us, whose thoughts you could never comprehend. Save your wisdom, old one, for your grandchildren. We've no need of it."

"Have you not?" The woman peered about at us all. "Have you not, indeed?" She shook her head. "You three are no wiser than babes, toddling from wall to wall for the first time. You think because you've lived forever, you know what it is to live.

"You"—she gestured to me—"you are youth without potential. You are strength without purpose. Eternal youth is not youth at all—it is frozen time, incapable of learning or growing. Our young people grow in bounds every day, in thought and body and spirit.

"And you," she said, turning to Serena, "you think you understand what it is to be a mother, a woman in her prime? But you have no yearnings for youthful days gone past, and you have no fear of the shriveling days to come.

"And the oldest of you is the least like us of all."

"Am I?" said Xinot. Her eyes were dark pebbles; her fingers twitched and twisted. She did not look human, true, but she did look wise, inscrutable, a creature of the night. I had always believed that Xinot knew things Serena and I only guessed at. That there were answers in her to questions the world hadn't thought to ask.

The old woman blinked at her, as if reconsidering what she was about to say. But then she gave a shake of her head and pointed a finger at Xinot. "You, crone, may be closer to the mysteries than your sisters. But you do not know the mystery of having lived a long life. You have not felt yourself change from day to day. You do not wake in the morning believing that you can run again, as fast as you ever did. You do not taste death in every last bite of food, feel him following as you shuffle about."

"Do I not?" said Xinot. "Do I not know death as well as you?"

In the silence, we all heard it. A gritty *snap*, as though a rusty pair of scissors was clanging shut. The old woman didn't move; I couldn't see her blink.

Then she drew in one long, shuddering breath. "You have seen much, all of you," she said. "But you will never understand what it is to live, to grow, to die. You will never understand the uncountable, priceless moments that make up those threads that you so casually spin, that toss us here and there with no thought for what's kind or what's fair. We are nothing to you." Then, low, "And you are nothing to us."

It was only what we had heard a dozen times in stories along the road: that we were separate from mortals; that we did not care. And it was true enough. There was no reason to lose my breath, hearing it again; there was no reason to hate this woman so.

Serena said, and there was such a bitterness in her voice, "What is it to you, then? Why should it matter what we know about Aglaia or about living, how wise or how ignorant we may be?"

"It doesn't," the woman said. "Not in any practical way. It's only that she's just gone off with him, and everyone is so overjoyed, and I know that something is not right." She nodded at me. "I'm not completely blind, maidy. I can sense the power that drips from you three. But you let her go to her fate anyway, so you cannot use it—or you choose not to, which comes to the same thing. And I cannot help wishing that you were different than you are, and resenting that you are not. And I am old, and I can speak my mind without fearing what you might do to me."

Xinot said, quiet, sure, "Resenting does no good."

The woman did not say anything for a moment, and then she sighed. "You are right, of course. No good at all." She turned back toward the door; she paused, saying over her shoulder, "I'll bring you a pot of stew, shall I? You needn't risk coming down into the inn while you stay." Her mouth quirked, and she laughed a dry laugh. "I don't suppose you'd care to be recognized by most people. Most wouldn't like you any more than I do."

She opened the door and left. After a few moments more, I went over and snatched my cloak from the floor, and I threw it around my shoulders. I sat by the fireplace with my hood pulled up, and my sisters left me alone.

We were not there when Aglaia and Endymion rode into the courtyard of his grand house. We were not there when he gave her the most elegant of his rooms or when he showered her with gowns, with jewels, with sweets. We didn't have to see her letting him take her hand as they planned their future. We didn't have to see the light she kindled in her eyes when he walked by or the way he looked at her, as if she was the answer to his dreams.

It wasn't our place, out there where the world was watching, where the stories were being spun.

It was ours to wait in the inn's dusky room, to do our work, to listen. We could have known all that was happening by running our hands along Aglaia's thread or by closing our eyes and finding it in the darkness, but there was no need.

The old innkeeper, Hesper, told us everything when she brought our meals. She kept her word; we didn't even leave our room to go down to the main floor where she served the other guests.

The stories Hesper brought were the ones heard by all the people of the city. Every word their heroes spoke, every touch and glance was passed along from maid to cook to delivery boy, and down through the sun-washed streets like rain.

They were in love. They were happy; they would be married in three days.

Rumor after rumor about the wedding circulated, gaining in splendor with each telling—there was to be a grand marriage feast; a largesse would be given, so huge that every beggar would be fed that day. The dancing would last far into the night. All the city's richest lords and ladies would attend, and all would wear shining new gowns, new fine-cut tunics.

Hesper didn't say anything more about us being powerless, but she relayed all these things dryly, giving us many looks. We ignored her; or at least, Xinot and I did. Serena smiled at the old woman and asked after her lad in the kitchen. We stayed silent as they chatted, and I remained irritated long after she had gone.

"Powerless," I muttered as we ate our noon meal the day before the wedding, seated on the floor around a plate of fruit, cheese, and bread. "I'd like to see a thing with more power than we have."

"Is it power if we never choose to use it?" said Serena, and I gave her a sharp glance, but she was calm, chewing a date.

"We choose not to use it *because* of how powerful it is," I said.

"Hmmm," said Serena.

Xinot said, "You are not suggesting that we do something?"

"No, of course not," said Serena.

"There's nothing to do, anyway!" I said.

Serena gave me a pacifying look. "I didn't say there was, Chloe."

"What could we do?" I said. "Kill Endymion before his time? Oh, maybe we should just take out his thread and cut it into pieces!"

"Chloe," said Serena.

I got to my feet and moved away from them toward the window. "What are we *doing* here?" I muttered.

Neither of them answered. When I turned, they were frozen, looking up at me. Xinot said, "We followed her this far."

Serena said, "She shines bright."

I sighed, and I shook my head. I peeked out through the shutters, where the sky over the city's white walls was sparkling blue. I didn't tell them we had to pack up, to run from this girl as fast as we could. I didn't want to, not any more than they did.

"What did you mean," I said suddenly, turning from the window to face Serena, "when you said I was only as old as you in years? What other way is there to be old?"

Serena blinked at me; she shook her head. "Never mind," she said. "I don't know what I meant."

Xinot said, gnawing calmly on a heel of bread, "Mortals count their age in years, Chloe. We are not mortals. Time does not do the things to us that it does to them."

"Yes," I said. "So?"

Serena said, "Xinot, it does not matter."

"So," said Xinot, "in years you are as old as Serena, as old as I am. In essence, though, you never will be. We will never be young, and you will never be old."

I said, "You sound like Hesper. Are you saying I am as inexperienced as Aglaia, that I know as little about the world as— as a newborn mortal?"

"Of course not," said Serena.

"Youth has its own wisdom," said Xinot. "And its own faults."

I thought about the way I never was the one who made our decisions. My voice was always third, and least. Then I thought about the way I had kept Aglaia's pain a secret from my sisters for so many weeks. I thought about how I was always protecting them, for fear they would lose themselves again, and a thread would break, and the darkness would scream, and our glory would disintegrate into nothing.

"You think I am the weakest, though," I said. When Serena began to make comforting sounds, I cut her off. "You don't realize how blind you both are. You don't realize how many problems you cause, how many times we would have been in real trouble if it hadn't been for me."

Xinot scoffed, "Name one."

I did it; I said the word none of us had uttered since that day: "Monster."

There was silence. My sisters were not looking at me, were not looking at each other. Xinot had dropped her hands with their bit of bread into her lap. Serena was staring blankly at our plate. *Just a cat,* I reminded myself. *How could they still be upset over just a cat?*

"That was my fault," said Serena softly. "Not Xinot's."

"She would have cut the thread," I said. "She *knew*."

It was a relief to say the words at last. Even as I saw the guilt creeping into their faces, I was glad to say it. I was glad to place the fault where it was due.

Xinot said, "Yes. Yes, Chloe, I knew."

I said, "I was the only one willing to stop it. I was the only one who wouldn't let us ruin everything."

There was a pause, and then Xinot said, "You spun the thread before Serena measured it, before I nearly cut it. If the end had happened, do you really think it would have had nothing to do with you?"

I remembered that thread, writhing in its wrongness, and the fury on Xinot's face. I remembered how close it had been— closer even than my sisters knew. I almost hadn't snatched it away in time. In my horror, I almost hadn't snatched it away at all . . . but then I did, didn't I? That was what counted. "If I did spin a faulty thread, I didn't mean to. And when I realized what was happening, I knew what to do. I was the only one of us who knew what to do."

I thought they weren't going to respond. Xinot had put

her bread back on the plate; Serena was twisting a date in her fingers, around and around. I didn't feel like eating anymore either. I pulled a chair over to sit by the window, leaning onto the sill. It had been so close, and he had been just a cat. Just one bright-eyed, soft-furred cat. And they thought me the weak one.

Xinot's words came from behind me, and they were low and hard. "You don't know everything."

I didn't turn to face her, but I muttered, and I know she heard, "Neither do you."

That night Aglaia came to visit us. Hesper showed her to our door. As she slipped in, we looked up from the thread, and we caught our breath. She was cloaked; she seemed another one of us, her hood pulled low over her face, strands of her golden hair peeking out at the edges.

When she'd closed the door behind her and pulled back her hood, she stood there looking from one of us to another, scrunching her face in thought. We waited, paused in our work. Xinot was perched at the end of our bed, her scissors held in one hand, the thread in another. It curled over to Serena, who was seated between the bed and the open window, and then stretched toward me, in the room's other chair before the fireplace, my spindle at my feet.

The thread gleamed, of course, a spider's web of starlight. Against our dark draped cloaks and darker eyes, it stood in greater contrast. A whisper, a fishing line, a flutter of a bird's wing.

At last Aglaia said, and her voice floated softly through our room like a shared thought, "I mean to kill him tomorrow night, after the wedding. He suspects nothing. I will be his heir, and any baby I bear after me."

Yes, we said.

She said, "Yes, it will be so?"

No, we said.

"No, it will not be so?"

No, we cannot tell you that.

Aglaia said, "You know his thread. You know the time and shape of its ending."

We cannot tell you that.

She demanded, "Do I succeed?"

We remained silent.

She looked about at us all, and I could see her anger, clear and sharp. Something twisted inside me, but there was nothing more to say, nothing more to do.

She said, and it was almost not a question, it was so heated, "Why are you *here*?"

We didn't try to answer her.

After a few long moments, she left us, without saying another thing.

Endymion's city had never seen such a wedding. It began with the sunrise, and it lasted long into the night. The rumors had all been true, though they did not begin to describe the pageantry this prince put on for the marriage to his destined bride.

There wasn't one grand feast, but four—one upon waking, one at midday, one at sunset, and a last at midnight, after the couple had gone to their marriage bed. There were honeyed figs and dates rolled in crushed nuts, sweet rolls and salty breads, lentil porridges, chickpea stews, lamb served with every sauce, fish so tender it crumbled in your mouth. The wine was everywhere; Hesper brought us a sampling, and though it didn't reach the heights of our wine in its glory days, it smelled of fresh spring grasses and tasted of sunshine.

The plays and the games began right after the morning feast. Puppet shows on street corners, dramas in the city squares. There were ball-throwing games and balancing games and all manner of sport—wrestling and racing, swordplay and javelin throwing. Children ran from one end of the city to the other, and their parents didn't try to stop them. Everywhere, bakers passed out sweets and brewers poured beer.

In the more sophisticated sections of the city, the greatest actors in the land performed comedies, and virtuosos sang ballads composed for this occasion, featuring the noble prince and his beautiful bride. Aglaia and Endymion sat on a platform at one end of the city's main square; they held hands all day long, and there were flowers in their hair. They watched jugglers juggle and acrobats leap. They danced, to drums and flutes and lyres, smiling and laughing as they stepped and spun.

In the afternoon, Endymion's men pledged their faith to

Aglaia. They knelt before her, and they kissed her fingers, and she smiled at them.

Before the sun went to bed, all the bells in the city rang, and all the revelers stopped what they were doing, put down their drinks, and looked to the sky. In the main square, Endymion bowed his head and held one arm around Aglaia. He had offered her this moment of silence to remember her parents, her older brother and her younger sister, all the people of her village who had so tragically not lived to see this day.

She stared straight ahead, our girl. Her eyes were dry, and she leaned into her new husband's embrace as though it were the only thing that mattered in the world. When the bells rang again, she turned to him, and she kissed him softly on the lips. He brushed a hand against her cheek, so gentle. Everyone watching could see the love for her in his eyes.

They ate their sunset meal as a bard sang of Endymion's greatest battles, of Aglaia's bright eyes, her neck, her skin. They danced again afterward, with each other, with the lords and ladies under the stars. The celebration was still in full swing when Endymion pulled his bride close and said something in her ear.

She ducked her head, smiling. He took her hand and they walked back through the streets, not bothering with horses or with a carriage. Their people stood aside for them, murmuring blessings, reaching out hands to touch Aglaia's skirt and the ends of her hair.

As they reached the prince's house, I took his thread from my bag and placed it on a little table that stood in one corner of our room. We gathered around it. We had been listening to it all that wedding day. The shutters were open; the curtains were drawn back. It was a new moon night; it was Xinot's night. It was so still, not even the stars were whispering. Xinot took the middle position in front of the thread, and she reached out her left hand to Serena, her right to me. We stood with our backs to the window, cloakless, our hair beginning to drift.

Endymion led Aglaia through his house, up stairs and down corridors, murmuring flatteries in her ear. She laughed softly, and her eyes sparked. They turned a corner, passed through a door, and entered his bedroom.

He let go of her hand to shut the door behind them, and she turned, waited for him, watched as he lifted his head to smile at her.

Fool. He did not know it, but we did. This was her night.

It was her destiny, and it was her due. We could not help her with it, but we could approve. We could lift his thread and hold it close as she smiled back at him, as she became exactly what he wanted her to be. As she drew her hair, bright as the stars, across one shoulder, and he stared. As she went to the table set with crystal goblets and the day's spring-smelling, sun-tasting wine.

She did not need us for the poison. She did not need us for anything. He could not see the powder she slipped into his glass; it was dim in the room, with only a banking fire and a dark-red lamp. He was not watching for it, anyway. He was not watching anything but her.

She didn't even need to kiss him again, the death that she gave him was so fast.

As his thread began to flicker, as it started shedding sparks, we placed it on the table and turned our backs, so that he would be alone at the end.

Twelve

IF SHE HADN'T BEEN AGLAIA—IF SHE HADN'T already won their hearts, received their pledges of faith, entered into their ballads—there might have been more questions about Endymion's death.

When she woke them in the middle of that night, though, with a scream that carried into the streets, bringing those who had finally gone to bed out of their homes again, their hearts racing, their nightdresses flapping in a chill wind—when she showed them Endymion's body, undressed, lying in their marriage bed, and she wept as though there was nothing left of her but her tears, her shaking hands, and her *pain*—when she begged them not to take him away, clinging to Endymion's house guard like a shivering leaf, reaching for the prince even as his soldiers lifted him up and carried him from the room—

there was not a person in the city who didn't believe her.

We heard it through our window, the whispering in the streets.

He was so happy, it overcame him.

His heart burst with the love.

At least he died knowing that she lived and that she had married him.

"He got what was coming to him, didn't he?" Hesper said, and we each smiled at her, just a bit. She chuckled darkly. "Good for her—and good for you, I suppose."

"We had nothing to do with it," Serena said.

"No more than you have to do with anything," Hesper said. "Still. It was well done. I heard the fear in her voice as she talked of him."

Aglaia kept to their marriage room, those long, hot days leading up to the funeral. I asked the sun to look in on her there, to keep her company. There was no need. My friend never left Aglaia's side if he could help it.

When they burned Endymion's body in a mighty pyre outside the city, everyone went, even the beggars, even Hesper. We sat alone in the city's strange, heavy silence, and we spun and measured and *sliced* to keep our hands busy, and she told us of it when she came back. Of the lords and ladies, dressed all in white, as sumptuously as they had for last week's wedding. Of the funeral cakes and the dark-red wine the soldiers passed out among the crowd. Of the children who ran beneath their feet, still nibbling on sweets, still laughing, though even that was muffled in the heat.

Our girl stood at the front of it all, in a gown so white it blinded, so you almost couldn't see the circles beneath her eyes, the pallor of her face. She was heartbroken, the people said, one after another after another. She only kept on for *his* sake, because he would want her to.

And for ours. It was an old clockmaker who said it first, Hesper told us. A little old man who spoke with such conviction that his words soon threaded all through the crowd as well.

She lives on for us. She is our princess. She will lead us now that he is gone.

When Endymion's body was only ash and the wood was heaps of coal, Aglaia turned from the smoldering remains and made her way back through the crowd, over the fields, into her city. She nodded at the people that she passed; she gave them her hand to touch.

I will care for you, it was reported that she said. *You are mine now.*

And then it was over. From that day on, Aglaia ruled her people from Endymion's house, and they followed her willingly. She didn't come to see us again; she didn't need our help. She never had. Her thread shone long and bright as ever.

So why did we linger?

The people cheered when Aglaia went into her city. We watched as well, our shutters open to ease the stifling air, our faces halfway hidden behind the pale-blue curtains that wafted, lazy, in the warm breeze. We did not let her see us.

We did not leave our room, except to ask Hesper for a bit of food now and again, when she forgot that we were there.

Aglaia came down through the streets many times in those last summer weeks, to shop in the colorful markets or to walk along the golden fields outside the city. She wanted the people to feel that she was touchable—not only a beautiful woman from a story, not only their princess, but one of them. Just a girl from a village.

She told them only a few weeks after the funeral that she was going to have the baby. She had to; she was showing, no matter how loose-fitting her clothes. They didn't question her. No one remarked on how fast she was growing. She had married their prince, so the child must be his, and it would lead them someday.

It was their dream come true; it felt to them the answer to Endymion's tragic death, the renewal of their hope, the beginning of a grand new tale. After she had told them, their love grew so bright that little children followed Aglaia whenever she came out of her home. They threw flowers to her, and they sang songs. She laughed and sang along. Her face glowed; her eyes shone; her hair rivaled the white stone walls for blinding glory.

We knew that she was happy. It should have been enough to send us back to our island. We should have left her there to her happiness, and we should never have bothered her again.

It was what the thread wanted of us.

When we worked, it tingled against our palms. It was growing impatient, the darkness that we served. We had left shelves of threads to grow lonely on our island; we had thrown ourselves into the path of this girl, when we were not the type who walked mortal paths. It had been a pulling sort of path, so it had made some sense for us to watch it for a time. But now things were settling and Aglaia's steps were slowing. There was nothing for us here anymore.

On windy nights, when we sat before our window and listened to the prayers sweeping through, we felt our magic, like a current, tugging us back to the sea. Especially in those dense summer days, the thought of our cool sea breeze prickled beneath my skin. When I closed my eyes, I could feel it dusting my cheeks with salt, whipping my hair to life, filling me with the deep, unending power of rolling waves. It missed me, and I missed it as a lonely man misses the touch of a hand on his. Remembering was loss; it was bitter pain.

Ah, but that was why we could not leave. Aglaia had come to her destiny; she had avenged her village and she was to lead her people. They would follow her. The men who had followed Endymion would follow her for his sake; and they would not betray her, for Aglaia and Endymion were more than mortal to these people. They were heroes; they charted their course through the stars.

But though Aglaia's steps were slowing, though she was settling, we could not quite believe her struggles were at an end. She was still beautiful. She still saw her world with bright, clear eyes.

And she was happy. Where was the pain?

We told ourselves it would only be until the baby was born. Six more months, and some weeks. We'd wait through the autumn and the rainy winter; when spring came, Aglaia would have the child, and we would leave.

We paid Hesper for our room, so we couldn't waver anymore. She counted the coins and wriggled her nose at them. "This isn't a pregnancy," she said, squinting at us. "This is a half year only."

Xinot shrugged; Serena smiled. I looked away from her, out the window.

Hesper counted the coins again. "Is it not his?" she said excitedly. "Is there some other lover, someone she deserves, who'll come and marry her soon enough?"

Serena said gently, "You know we can't tell you that."

"Can't?" said Hesper. "Or won't?"

Serena only shook her head.

"Ah, well. Life's more fun that way." Now that Endymion was dead, now that Aglaia was happy, even Hesper thought our world a fairer place.

It was a long winter, or so it seemed to us. We worked more than we had in many ages, to keep from thinking, to keep from screaming great earth-shattering screams at our confinement.

We took shifts at the window in turn, depending on whose moon it was. There was so little space to lean out and breathe the darkness, and we each wanted it all to ourselves. So we split it into thirds: my turn was from the new moon until it was two-thirds full; Serena's went through the full moon until it was one-third waned; and Xinot came back to the empty sky again. It was difficult, those other two-thirds of the month, not to see the stars, only to hear the prayers that managed to sneak in on a draft. But the joy of having the sky to myself for the other third nearly made up for it. To see my moon, glittering and fresh, soft with her potential—it reminded me of who I was, of what I loved.

We also got into the habit, as the months drew on, of tossing Xinot's fish bones when we grew especially bored.

We'd sit in a circle near the fire, as we had when we'd tossed the bones for Aglaia. It didn't matter the time of day: a pause in our work, an empty moment in the middle of the night, after a meal. One of us would move to the floor, and the others would follow, and Xinot would reach into her pocket for the clattering things.

She'd toss them, and we'd lean over to watch as they scattered. We'd wait. The darkness always came; it rushed through us, and we knew the words we spoke were true fortunes.

Snow of ash.

Earth of wind.

Silent screams and a shrieking silence.

They weren't anything we could understand—not even us, not even Xinot, with her whirling eyes, her knowing fingers.

The tangling comes undone, one of us would say. Or else, *It is an end. The world stops spinning. The stars go out.*

And then, always together, with one voice, *We will be to blame.*

You may wonder why we kept tossing the things, when

they gave us such a prophecy. We drew no joy from it. We shivered with the horror, and the guilt at this unknown blame pinched us with cold fingers.

Part of it was the truth of it—we couldn't deny the power in those bones. And part was that there was nothing else we could do. Even as we knew that every prophecy would be the same, each time we tossed them we couldn't help hoping that the bones would tell us something new about Aglaia, some reason to believe that her *pain* was gone for good.

That spring, as Aglaia's belly grew round, full as Serena's moon, we tossed the bones every day, and then twice a day, though nothing changed. We did not speak to one another anymore; the tune we hummed as we worked was thin and sharp. We stood by our window, watching Aglaia's city waking up to the year, stirring with happy anticipation of her baby. We were not of them. We never are, of course, but that spring we felt as far away as if we'd never left our island, as if a breaking sea and hours of empty land separated us from the crowd, and not only some slim blue curtains and a row of wooden shutters.

Hesper had been swept up in it as much as anyone. She smiled as she came to bring us food or take our dishes. She even whistled, though she couldn't get much sound through her wrinkled lips. "Won't be long now!" she said, winking at us. "Not by the measure of your coin!" She still held out hope that some long-lost beau was about to come riding into the city any day, to claim Aglaia as his own and take her away with him.

Even Serena had stopped chatting much with our inn-keeper. She smiled back, but weakly, and once Hesper had gone we returned to peering out the window or working at our thread or reading our bones for the fourth, the fifth time that day. Or Xinot watched the fire dance. Or Serena knit away at some useless project, with colorful yarn she'd bought from Hesper. Or I closed my eyes and listened.

I didn't tell my sisters, but I'd begun to read Aglaia's thread in the dark space behind my eyelids. Not her future; only to find out what she was doing right at this moment, whether she was well. I'd shut my eyes and reach for it, the bright swirl that was her. It would twist and turn, and I would see her, sitting in some city council; I would hear her, discussing nursery plans for the baby with the women of her house. She was still happy. She hadn't forgotten her village or her family, but she looked to the future. She would live her life for this child.

One night, after winter had gone for good, when the wheat was tall and the narcissus were flowering and beckon-ing the city's young and pretty out beyond its walls, Aglaia left Endymion's house to go out into the fields.

I was spinning, and I almost didn't notice that she'd gone. But I'd gotten into the habit of checking on her, even while I was busy with something else, and when there was a pause in our humming, when I was reaching for the next strand, as I blinked, I saw her slipping out a gate to the west. I smelled the wind along her hair, and I tasted the tears along her cheeks.

I finished the thread I'd started, but when Serena had measured it, when Xinot had *sliced*, I pulled the beginning of the next one out of my sisters' hands and tucked it into my basket along with my spindle.

"What is it?" Serena asked.

I shook my head at her. "Nothing to worry about. I'm going out."

"Out?" she said.

"Yes."

I stood from my place by the window. The moon had only just begun to wax; it was an icing of white on an invisible cake.

"You might be seen," said Serena.

"No one will see me," I said. I took my cloak from where it draped along our bed. "There's something I need to do."

"Alone?" said Serena.

"Yes," I said.

"Chloe," Xinot said. I turned to her, tying the cloak around my neck. "You can tell us. We aren't going to stop you."

"No?" I considered her.

"You may be the youngest," she said, "but if you say that you need to go, then we will let you go."

"Of course we will let you go," said Serena. "Chloe, what is it?"

I said, "Aglaia has left the city. I don't know if there will be another chance to see her, and I need to tell her something. One more time, I need to talk to her."

I tugged my hood up; I pulled my cloak snug around me.

I'd forgotten that I liked this; I liked the mysteriousness of it, the shadows it threw upon my face.

Serena touched my shoulder; she had come over next to me. When I looked at her, she handed me a soft, squishy thing. It was a hat, small as a cat's head. "For the baby," my sister said. "Will you give it to her?"

I nodded.

"You could tell her we've tossed the bones," said Xinot.

I had to laugh. "*A sharpened wine,*" I said. "*A watery knife.* It will do her good to hear our discoveries."

Xinot's small grin showed one jagged tooth. "Go safe, Chloe."

I pulled Serena's gift beneath my cloak. I nodded once again, and left.

I found her at the top of a hill, standing before the empty stretch of land where they had burned Endymion last summer. The farmer had not sown his wheat here. All around us, grains bobbed, silver in the faint moonlight. Here the earth was black and bare. I thought there was maybe still a whiff of ash in the dust.

She was bundled up in a thick tunic and a warm cloak. She stood a bit hunched, her arms drawn around herself and her head bent low. She didn't look up as I came over beside her, but she said, "Hello, Chloe."

I suppose she knew my scent, the touch of my presence, as well as I knew hers. We had sat, the only thinking things, in the middle of an empty ocean, and we knew the shape of each other.

I said, "We are no use, Aglaia. I have no prophecy for you."

She shivered, and she drew even farther into her cloak. "I did not expect one."

"I don't know why we're still here."

"I wasn't going to ask it."

I shook my head, looking out over the remains of Endymion's pyre, seeing the fire leaping, crumbling him to bits. I wished again that I could have done it myself, with my own strangling hair or teeth. "We should have left after you killed him. That was the purpose of your journey, wasn't it? And we should have left after we had found you, when we knew there was nothing we could do to help. And we should have never followed you."

Aglaia gave a little laugh. "I've given up trying to understand what you do."

I squinted up at my moon. "We serve the darkness."

"Whatever that means," Aglaia said.

"It means we spin and we measure and we cut, and we do not interfere."

"Ah." She glanced at me; her eyes flashed beneath her hood, and I wondered if that was how I had looked, questioning the oracle. "You put that spell on me, though. Was that not interfering?"

"It was not meant to be. You were meant to leave and get on with your life." I sighed. "We never mean to become involved."

She said, soft, "But you do anyway?"

I said, "My sisters do, or they have."

"And was it such a bad thing?"

"Yes," I said. "Yes, it was a very bad thing."

We were silent. She went back to hunching over herself, staring at the ground. It was a cool, clear night. The stars shone, pinpricks, and the wheat rustled now and again, a calm sea surrounding our hilltop island.

I thought that Aglaia was crying, and I asked, "Do you regret it?"

"What?" she said. "Killing him?"

"Yes."

Hard and certain, she answered, "No. I don't regret it."

"Then why did you come all the way out here tonight?"

There was a pause, and I wasn't sure she was going to answer me. But then she said, "Do you know what I hate him for the most? I mean beyond what he did to my family and my village?"

I shook my head.

"I hate that he made it my fault."

"But it wasn't."

"He wanted me. I refused him. He destroyed everything I loved."

"That was him," I said. "It wasn't you."

"Yes," said Aglaia. There was a matter-of-factness to her voice that made me want to do something—take her hand, maybe, or beg her to look at me, to stop saying such things. "It was him, and I know it wasn't me. But it also was, Chloe. Even though I know it wasn't, I can't quite believe it."

We stood, unspeaking, for another minute. Then I said, "If

you must blame somebody other than him, Aglaia, you could blame us."

She tilted her head, as though listening to something, and I could see that she had shut her eyes. One hand was to her belly. She was as still as a painting. After a moment, she opened her eyes again. "When I am thinking straight, I know that it doesn't actually matter," she said, and her voice was light again, musical. "Whether it's his fault or my fault or your fault, it's over. He is dead, and I killed him; and that was his destiny, so you killed him as well."

"Well done, us," I muttered.

I wasn't watching, so I didn't notice her reaching for me until she had taken my hand, until she was pulling it over toward her belly.

"Listen to this," she whispered.

The baby was rolling, and I couldn't really hear anything, but I closed my eyes as she had done, and I tilted my head, and I felt it move, the little living thing. I forgot, for a moment. Endymion, who to blame, *pain*. I even ceased to remember who I was; I didn't even think of my wool, or my moon, or our glory.

This baby had no thread. It moved in darkness; it knew nothing of the world. It was pure, unspun potential. I was smiling at it, without knowing why.

"And this is why it doesn't matter either," came Aglaia's voice, from above, as the baby would hear it. "Endymion is gone, and my child will live."

The baby settled. I stepped back, opening my eyes.

"Still," said Aglaia, "when I am not thinking straight, I hate him for it."

I watched her blinking hard, hugging herself again. Maybe this was the pain we had been looking for. Maybe the oracle had predicted Aglaia's ongoing pain at the raiding of her village, and nothing more.

She said, "I came out here tonight to let it go. I wanted to think about him one more time, to be bitter and angry, and to hurt. When the baby comes, I want to look forward, not back. I want to choose for the future, not weep over the past."

I nodded.

"It won't be long now, Chloe," Aglaia said. She touched her belly again, gently.

"I know," I said. "Here." I pulled out Serena's gift and handed it to her. "We can't do anything useful with our power, but this is for your baby, when it comes. And I wanted to say that I was sorry, for anything we have done to harm you, and that I wish you a long and happy life."

Aglaia rubbed the hat between her fingers, feeling its softness. She smiled at me. "Is that a real wish, Chloe? Will it come true?"

I tried to smile back. "I don't know. We cannot—"

"I know," she interrupted. "You cannot interfere."

"Yes."

"Well." She looked down at the hat for a moment, and then, shocking me, she turned and stepped toward me, and she hugged me. "As one powerless creature to another, then, thank you."

She pulled back, and I saw the peacefulness in her face,

the acceptance of the fate she'd found. I could have closed my eyes and read the future in her thread. I could have done that at any time, to know for sure which way her path bent, whether she got to keep this happiness.

I reached out, and as Serena might have done, I tucked a strand of our girl's hair back into her hood. It wouldn't do any good, to know the ending. "We'll leave after the baby is born," I said, and I meant it this time.

She said, "Farewell, then, Chloe."

I whispered, "Farewell, Aglaia."

Then I turned, and I left her there, to feel bitter and angry and hurt that one last time. *Please,* I begged the stars, the wind, my moon. *Please let it be the last time.*

The baby came only a few weeks after that.

Of course they were not ready for it. They had thought she had several weeks yet to go, though she was as round as an overfed pig and as slow-moving. Their faith in her strained somewhat, knowing that she had gone into labor so early; the midwives, especially, muttered to themselves and cast one another meaningful looks.

But she was theirs; they would not give up on her now. If she said it was an early birth, they would believe her. Anyway, who would they have if they didn't have her? Their prince had loved her; all knew that. She was what they had left of him, and her child was their hope.

That night we spun only one thread. It was a long labor; it began early in the morning and went far into the dark. I held one hand ready at the spindle, the other hovering over my basket, waiting for the wool to call out the baby's birth.

We closed our eyes, and we were there with her, screaming as she screamed, rejoicing in her joy. She was in pain, but this was the best kind—she gave herself to it freely, loving it, loving what it would bring her. Our Aglaia did not shrink from difficult things. She would birth this child, and she would never tell it what its father had been. She would live a lie so it could grow up strong and free. She would watch it rule this city; she would never ask for another thing, as long as she could give this baby the world.

She screamed, and she pushed, and as the sun was blinking open his eyes, asking me whether she had done it yet, my fingers twitched, and I drew out the very first strand.

We began to sing as the wool went onto the spindle. It was the song we had heard Aglaia humming in this same room. A song of life, of long summer days. It was the song that Aglaia was hearing too, as her baby's head poked out into the air, as he drew his first breath, and then another, as his screams joined hers.

I spun, and I sang, and I passed this newest thread over to my sisters. I did not need to force misgivings away, not for this. I did not need to remind myself of my love of our work or to block out everything that was not the darkness.

The patterns were right, in the end; destiny resulted in glory, in light, in babies being born. What did death matter, when babies were born?

His eyelashes were perfect. His lips were sweet as the

dawn. He curled his fingers, and his mother wept and kissed his knuckles.

Serena was smiling as she measured the thread.

Xinot drew out her blades with her age-old smoothness, and her scratchy voice hummed and hummed.

An instant before the scissors closed, we paused, all three of us, and our song bent, and shattered.

Then *snap*.

I let my spindle fall; Serena dropped her hands. Aglaia's baby boy's thread coiled in Xinot's palm.

There it was, the word that had faded through these last few months, but never completely away, never enough that we couldn't hear its echo.

Pain.

For the rest of Aglaia's golden thread, the memory of this one would torture her.

Serena gave a soft cry. She turned from it; she put her face in her hands and her head to the wall.

I reached out a finger to touch the end of the thing. I murmured, "How long?"

Xinot was cupping it as though it were a warm egg—or a kitten, come in from the storm. She shook her head. "Not long. A few days, maybe."

Such a beautiful snippet. It isn't true that the shorter they are, the brighter they shine. But this one was so glorious, it hurt even us to look at it.

The darkness was all around it, loving it, waiting for its end.

PART THREE

Thirteen

THE BABY BEGAN TO SICKEN ALMOST AT ONCE. We heard it from Hesper, of course, and she did not speak to us dryly, not about this. There were tears in her eyes, and her voice was hollow.

"Can't you do anything?" she asked, hugging a pitcher of water she'd brought for us against her chest.

I turned my face from her. It was Xinot who said, "I thought you believed that we were powerless."

Hesper laughed, a wet gulp. "Now, you wouldn't listen to an old lady like me."

We smiled, but we had no comfort for her.

"Please, mistresses," she said. "It's only a *baby*. And she's only a little girl."

There was a silence; it went on and on. Serena said, quiet and quieter, "We know."

"You spun the thread," said Hesper. It was almost a question.

I whispered, "Yes."

She placed the pitcher on our little table. She rubbed a hand across her eyes and shuffled to the door. She paused; she said, "It shouldn't bother me anymore. There have been so many children, so many mothers in pain. I should be armored against these things by now."

I saw that Serena could not speak, and Xinot was making the fish bones clatter in her pocket. I said, "Yes, Hesper. So should we."

She left us to our silence.

We did not spin the thread, those days the baby lived. I do not know what would have happened if we had. We hardly spoke or moved. We heard each of the baby's cries. We tasted each of Aglaia's tears. We felt the whole city mourning the child that had been its hope.

We waited for her. She would come.

She would tell us we were to blame.

We would nod. We would let her words sink into us, let their barbs pierce our organs, their poisons slide through our veins. We would feel her *pain* for the rest of our forever. This was the fulfillment of the prophecy we had made every time we had tossed the bones. We had thought it had nothing to do with Aglaia, but it did. The pattern was wrong. Fish flew; seas boiled. The world could not be the way it was.

We waited, knowing there was nothing to be done. There was never anything to be done.

I envied mortals, that week the child lived. I envied the way you think that you have a choice in how you live, which path you walk toward death. It is an illusion, but it is a happy illusion. I envied you your blindness, and I wished more than I had ever wished for anything that my sight might be taken away as well.

I did not want to know anymore. I did not want to hear this story; I did not want to accept this fate.

My sisters and I were nothing, that week, but women waiting. We sat, we looked at one another, and we waited.

And then she came to us.

She did not come cloaked this time. She had no need to hide her movements; everyone in this city was her friend, and she rode up with the prince's house guard to the door of the inn. She left them there and followed Hesper up the stairs to our room, hair unbound and tangled over her shoulders, shadows under her eyes, her baby moaning quietly in her arms.

"His name is Taddeo," our girl told us. Hesper closed the door and hovered behind her, watching us anxiously.

The tip of a nose poked out of the blankets. We could not help it; we went over to him, and we peered in. So scrunchy, so small, so helpless. Serena's hat was pulled snug over his head. "Taddeo," said Xinot. "A brave little boy."

"I call him Tad," said Aglaia, "and he is brave, but he is not strong enough to win out against this thing."

We did not look at her, only at him, only at his sweet mouth, his soft skin.

She said, putting her face close to the baby, near our ears, "Show me his thread."

We shook our heads.

"Yes," she said. "You will. Show me my son's thread."

Serena went over to one of my packs; she rummaged a bit. We do not lie about such things, yet the thread she brought over to Aglaia was long and strong and bright.

Aglaia blinked. We held our breaths. "No," she said. "That's not his thread. That's mine."

So Xinot reached into her pocket, not the left one where she kept her fish bones and her blades, but the other one, the one I'd never seen her use before, and she drew out little Tad's thread. It shone there on her palm.

Aglaia stared. She was not surprised. She did not cry; she didn't even blame us for it. "I see," she said. "Yes. That one is his."

She lifted her child to her face. She kissed his forehead, and he wriggled his nose, but weakly. He was pale, even paler against the bright colors of his hat. We had not seen his eyes.

"Would you like to hold him?" she said, offering him to Serena.

Oh, what a question. Serena opened her arms for the baby.

It was so fast. Our girl must have planned this out; she must have readied herself for it, because she did not hesitate or fumble. As Taddeo settled into Serena's hold, Aglaia snatched her long thread from my sister's fingers and slid her other hand into Xinot's left pocket, grabbing the deadly shears.

She backed away from us. Hesper, still watching wide-eyed near the door, stepped to the side. Xinot lunged for the scissors. I dove for the thread. Before either of us could reach her, Aglaia drew her fingers along her life, held it tight, and *snapped* the blades closed.

Her childhood, her last few years tumbled to the floor among the dust.

We stopped, arms out. Taddeo whimpered.

Aglaia reached for the baby's snippet, and Xinot let her take it. She held one end to the other—Tad's death to the beginning of the rest of her life. The threads sparkled, separate, unconnected.

She tied them together. They untwisted themselves the next moment.

She put the ends in her mouth—we gasped, sure of disaster—and then she held them together, pressing, hoping they'd stick.

"Chloe," she said, looking up at me as they each coiled into one palm again.

I said, not recognizing my own voice, "What is it, Aglaia?"

But I knew, of course.

She said, "Help me," and she held out the threads. There was no anger, no bitterness in her face. There was only a deep, trembling sea and a thing I could not bear—an unquenched spark of hope. Looking at her, I knew finally the truth I had been ignoring, the thing I had not allowed myself to say, to think. Aglaia was not my acquaintance; she was not my comrade. It was much more terrible than that. For months and months now, I had loved this girl, with as hard and fiery a love as I kept for our waves, our stars, our glorious threads.

I had told my sisters about the baby because I loved her. I had searched out the oracle in her cave because I loved her, and I had followed her all this way because I could not bear to let her go when there was maybe something I could still do for her.

I had given myself so many other reasons—protecting my sisters, anger at a false prophecy, answering the pull of the darkness. I hadn't believed in this love, so I'd been able to think that nothing had changed, that I was the same uncaring Chloe, whose only passions were her work, and the glances of handsome men, and the smell of the sea wind. Who would rather kill a thousand mortals than betray her calling.

Then this moment came, when she was asking me for help again, as she had done so many times before, and she was looking at me as though we were friends. And her little Tad was barely breathing in Serena's arms, and Aglaia's hands were stretched out, offering her chance at happiness, her escape from a lifetime of pain to me.

I don't know if my sisters would have stopped me. Serena was holding Tad; she could not keep me back. Xinot might have. I heard her starting to growl a warning as I snatched the threads from Aglaia's hands. But I didn't wait long enough to find out what dire consequences this might bring. As Aglaia had *snapped* her thread before we could blink, so I took Tad's snippet and the longer half of his mother's coil in one quick motion, and I twisted them together, end to end.

Tad's was so short, I used a good length of Aglaia's to make up for it. I wound it around and around her baby's thread. I reached for the power fizzling along each minute strand. As I do when I shape and spin, I fell into our glory, and I told it what to do. My fingers buzzed; the power swept round me like a cloak billowing with wind. I said a word I didn't know I knew. It echoed, even in our small inn room. It boomed, and something burst into flames—my mind, my hands, the threads back in our house at the edge of the sea. Yes, as the snippet and the long golden length grew warm in my hands, and two turned into one, I thought I felt a great fire burning, all our work going up in a blaze.

Then something screamed—the darkness, I suppose, as I wrenched its patterns out of place, as I tied a knot and sealed it, as I pulled the new thread tight, and it *held*.

What I make, what I twist and tie, stays made.

The fire faded; the thread cooled. Aglaia's life, nearly done, piled on the floor. Tad's, long and golden, pooled and shimmered in my hands.

Aglaia held out her arms for her child. The darkness's scream was rising into a shriek. As the girl went over to our bed and lay down on it, already breathing shallower, sweating and shivering, Taddeo opened his eyes.

Oh, Aglaia. Clever girl, with such clear sight. She knew exactly how far she'd lived; she knew how much life she had to give.

The boy's eyes were a dark, deep green, the color of the sea before a storm. I wanted suddenly to be standing out on our empty rocks, overlooking the endless waves. Tad held out a tiny hand, and Aglaia fit her pinkie into the folds of his palm.

"Thank you," she whispered, kissing his face, once and again and again. "Chloe, thank you."

Hesper appeared at the head of the bed; she sat by the pillow, smoothing Aglaia's hair from her face.

"This is our mystery," she said to us, as Aglaia smiled softly, as her eyes began to close. "This is what you cannot touch, not even you, old one."

"No," said Xinot. "We cannot."

We ignored the way the world was shuddering beneath our feet. We paid our darkness's panicked demands no attention, not as Hesper murmured a good-bye song, not as Aglaia faded, and then faded even more.

She was leaving us. As Serena's children had left her, as Monster had left, Aglaia was taking a path we could never follow her down.

She breathed. She cradled her son's small head. Hesper whispered something in her ear, and the thread she had dropped to the floor sparked and shimmered, and fizzled into the dark.

She was gone.

Her eyes were closed—no more clear sight, no more pain. Only her beauty was left now, and that would go soon enough.

Our girl. We had followed her all the way to this, the only real end.

I had only just found my heart, and I had shattered it instantly. I had only just realized my love for this girl, and now she would never open her eyes; she would never again speak to me. The sea that had been on my friend's face was inside me now, breaking and breaking, in wave after endless wave. And I could do nothing to stop the break, and I could only feel my heart's shattered pieces, burning and tearing so much there was nothing whole left of me.

I stood with my sisters beside the bed, shattered, breaking. We looked down at the boy that she had died to save. He was blinking up at us. There was color already on his cheeks.

In my hand, his thread was flashing bright red and sharp yellow. He had reached the place where his snippet met what was left of Aglaia's life.

I don't need to tell you that we had no idea what was going to happen now. Of course we had never done such a thing as this. I did not know if it was even possible, to give away an unused life.

Taddeo was opening and closing his mouth, making little sounds. Hesper reached over to touch his head, but then pulled back and drew away from the bed.

"He's *burning*," she said, and there was fear on her face.

The baby's skin was glowing now, a bright, shining pink. He lifted his hands, spreading his fingers wide and then scrunching them tight. He kicked his feet.

I held my palms out flat, and the thread writhed on them.

And then Tad started to grow.

It was only a little stretching, a bit of rounding out, at first. He was a baby, still, but healthy, and his eyes opened wide and he smiled, cooing. His hair grew longer, yellow like his mother's, wavy like his father's. He began to cry as teeth edged into his mouth, and he wailed, shaking his arms as they grew.

He quieted, and he blinked at us.

"Is it over?" Hesper said.

We shook our heads. The thread was shooting off green sparks; it was only beginning.

"His clothes," Serena breathed. She rushed over to the bed and grabbed her hat from the boy's head. With one fluid twist, she threw his blanket to the floor. She moved her clever fingers, unfastening this, tugging at that, and as she drew off his shirt and slipped the cloth from his bottom, he started to blur around the edges, and we heard a high, keening noise.

Serena stepped back hurriedly.

The threads that I spin are essentially all the same width. Time does not speed or slow for you mortals, not objectively. But I had needed to wrap so much of Aglaia's thread around the end of Tad's that where the two met, there was a knot many times the size of a normal thread. Tad had reached that knot, and time was moving much faster for him than usual.

We could not help him. We were afraid of trying to touch him, even; we only stood watching, the four of us, and we hoped.

He was shifting quickly now, his skin, his bones extending through months and then years. All around him was a fuzziness, a mist of muted color. We could see a brightness at the center, where the boy transformed.

It seemed to take forever; for him it did. For us, it really wasn't more than a few minutes before the mist faded away and the keening ended, leaving the hollow sobbing of a frightened child.

We went over next to the bed and looked down at him. I closed my eyes as the room spun around. I had done this, the thing that would topple us all. I had taken the world as it was and turned it into what I thought it should be.

Aglaia's son was a baby no longer. He had grown five, nearly six years. He curled up under her chin, in the curve of her arm, and he was so big he was almost sliding off the bed.

After a moment Hesper said slowly, as though she couldn't quite believe she was speaking, "I have an old tunic from when I first brought my lad in off the streets. He'll need it." She paused. "Won't he?"

I couldn't think to reply. Serena was kneeling by the bed, stroking the child's hair as he cried. Xinot said, "Yes. You should fetch that," and Hesper slid away, out of the room.

"He's so old," I said. "How can he already be so old?"

Xinot said, "How can he still be alive?"

I looked at her. There had been no accusation in her words, only wonder. Whether or not she would have stopped me from tying the threads, she did not blame me for this. I watched her watching Serena and Tad, and there was a fire in her like the fire that had burned as I twisted the ends together, and I thought too that whether or not she would have stopped me, she had not wanted to.

Her head was also tilted, though, listening, and her legs were braced against the floor, and I knew that she could feel it, the way the ground was buckling. This was much worse than when she had almost *sliced* a thread at the wrong point. This was far beyond Serena's tense silence when she had mourned her children. We would not get away from this by running, or with a reprimand.

We had done it—*I* had done it, the thing that would tear everything apart. For a girl to die before her time was one thing. Aglaia's death was wrong; it made the darkness shudder, but it was not unheard of, for a mortal to leave her thread too soon.

For a baby to be given a whole long life, when he hadn't any to start with, for a week-old child to grow five years in two minutes, was something else.

I lifted my chin; Xinot nodded, sharp. Then we each took one of Serena's arms, and we pulled her from the bed to stand. I caught her eye, and I knew that she was with us too, in this thing—that she wouldn't have tried to stop me, not even knowing the end. Xinot reached around and grabbed my other hand, and we leaned into one another.

At last we closed our eyes, and the darkness was waiting for us.

It wanted to know what we could possibly be thinking. Its web was unraveling fast, and we were at fault, we who were pledged to keep it safe.

We did not make excuses; there were none. We did not say, *A life for a life*; we know that's not a fair trade.

The darkness said, in its wordless way, that it had never lied to us. We knew what it was. We knew its rules; we had known them since the beginning.

We know, we said. *We have chosen this knowing.*

It told us that the boy could not live. If he lived, everything would end.

It was angry at us. It was furious, and the heat of it poured through us, as it had after Monster died. It was showing us just exactly what we had put at risk: the beautiful tangle of fate that we had always loved.

Here was what it could not realize, though, what I never would have believed even if I had read this fortune a thousand times: It was too late for us. We had made our choice—to love a mortal more than anything, more than our darkness. We would end the world for the sake of this girl, as she had ended her life for the sake of her son.

Was it betrayal? Oh, yes, I knew it was.

But I did not care. I loved her, and as our magic raged, I could feel my heart breaking still, and I could feel my anger growing too, at all Aglaia had endured, at all she'd given up.

The clouds were gathering fast outside our window, much faster than clouds should gather. There were ominous lights in the sky—not lightning flashes, but burning pits of fire, where no fire should be. The people were beginning to come out into the streets, to understand that the world was at an end.

We had predicted this, after all. *Rain of fire. An end to all patterns.*

The darkness told us, and it was as though it was granting us a gift, that there was one thing we could do to save it, still.

We didn't ask what that was; we already knew. We always know.

We would not do it.

It shrieked at us that everything would end!

We knew. We would not do it.

It reminded us, and there was a desperate edge to it, that we were sworn, that this was what we were, its keepers, its protectors. We couldn't let it die.

We opened our eyes. We stepped back from one another and dropped our hands. We were not listening anymore.

The boy was crying, and the people were screaming. Hesper came rushing up with her lad's old tunic; she went over to the window and threw the shutters wide, holding tight to the sill as the deep tremors we had been feeling began to shake the surface of the world.

"What is it?" she cried. "What's happening?"

The world is ending, we said.

She looked at us with horror. "Is it your fault?"

Yes, we said.

She screamed, and we almost couldn't hear her over the crashing, over the running and yelling and thunder, "You have to make it stop!"

We only looked at her. Serena went back to the bed, back to soothing Aglaia's son.

"Can't you make it stop?" cried our innkeeper.

We can, Xinot and I said. *But we won't.*

"You must!"

It was terrible, but it was thrilling, to stand beside my sister as the city crumbled and to do nothing—just to stand and let it fall. We said, rejoicing in it, *We won't.*

Hesper watched as we knelt beside Serena. I touched Aglaia's cooling hand; we would be joining her soon enough. Xinot hummed a tune of cataclysms, of breaking points, of beautiful horrors.

I had never known an end could be beautiful like this. It was, though. All of us together would fall into the void. All of us together would go to a place we could not imagine; together we would finally die.

We paid no attention as Hesper lowered herself down next to us, leaning on her cane. She was crying, but silently; the tears rolled down her wrinkled face as she lifted the boy with shaking hands and helped him into the tunic. She pulled herself up to sit on the bed, settling Tad onto her lap. He had stopped crying at last. He snuggled against her, his thumb tucked into his mouth. She slid something from a pocket on her dress, where Xinot would have kept her shears.

She held it close against Tad's neck.

It was a small, very sharp knife.

Fourteen

"IT'S HIM, ISN'T IT?" HESPER WHISPERED. "HE'S what you won't give up."

We didn't answer her, but she could read it in our eyes as we stared; she could hear it in our breaths that caught and stuck, in our suddenly frantic heartbeats.

She said, and it was almost kind, "You cannot destroy the world for the sake of one child."

I made the beginning of a noise, I don't know what it was— some almost-cry, some almost-scream. Hesper held the knife steady against the boy's throat with one hand, stroking his hair again and again with the other. She said, as I had so many ages ago to Monster, "Good-bye, little one. Go well into the dark."

She kissed his forehead. She drew in the breath that was to end his.

I made that sound again, that almost-sound.

There was something in it that did not fit with the angry joy we had been feeling. There was something in it, so lost, so helpless, that did not ask for vengeance or fairness. It did not ask for anything. It only cried out, because there was nothing else that it could do. Again, again, there was nothing that I could do.

Aglaia, I thought, the moment before her boy died. *Aglaia, I am sorry. I have failed you after all.*

I am not proud of it, but I closed my eyes. I did not want to see the final fragment.

There in the darkness behind my eyelids, Aglaia was looking at me. That flashing blue, that sweeping gold. The sure set of her mouth and her raised chin. She'd lost a world and kept on going. She'd done the impossible—found our island, tricked a prince, saved a child that fate itself had abandoned.

She had died to save this boy. She had *died*, and my heart had broken—was still breaking—would never stop breaking. And I was giving up?

One soft cry.

My sisters and I had linked hands, instinctively, as Hesper had pulled out her blade. We were as close as we ever are, in our dread, in our sure knowledge of the end.

It only takes one breath to kill a boy, but thoughts travel much faster than that, and my sisters knew mine.

That almost-sound rose within me, shrilled, pierced into a mountain-shattering *shriek*.

Hesper hesitated, only a bare wisp, but it was enough for

Xinot to *twist;* her arm shot up and the knife spun through the air, arched over our heads, and clattered to the floor behind us.

Serena was on her feet, holding her fists tight before her, looking off at nothing, at where our darkness was. We watched her, all of us still. I had only known that we must not let the boy die, not without trying to save him. That was what I had thought; that was what my sisters had responded to. I did not know what Serena had in mind, but I did not doubt that there was something. She was the most powerful thing, standing there—a mother enraged, lifting a loaded cart with her own two hands; running a thousand miles without a stop; untying a melded, sea-soaked knot and pulling a drowning child to the sun.

We could hear Hesper breathing, harsh. Xinot and I were trembling, as though we stood at the edge of a very steep something.

Serena said, and that power was full in her voice, *No, there must be another way.* She paused; she shook her head. *No,* she said again, surer. *It isn't the boy's death that you need; you need him not to have lived at all.*

The tremors shaking the city quieted for a moment; there was a questioning sort of break in the crashing thunder.

She went on, gaining certainty as she spoke. *You need him not to live a full human life, out where he would tear apart your patterns. You need him to go away from it all. He cannot influence other threads; he cannot change the world. He must be separate.*

Serena paused, and in the silence we heard the people's screams, louder now that the other noise had calmed. *You need us to remove him from the tangle, as a bug from a spider's web. We can do that.*

Now I understood; the spark caught and started to burn. I got to my feet as well. I took Serena's hand, stared where she stared. *Yes,* I said into the face of our darkness, *we can do that.*

Xinot said, a low hiss from the bed, *We'll take him with us.*

I said, *He'll never leave our island.*

Serena said, *He'll never fall in love.*

Or kill a man.

Or ask a powerful question.

Or answer one.

He'll never lead his people.

He'll never have a child.

Or a farm.

He'll be nothing, we said, we promised, we prophesied. *We swear it.*

Hesper said, in quite a soft voice, so that we almost did not hear, "By the gods, you don't know what you are doing."

We ignored her. Serena asked our darkness, *Is it a deal?*

There was a flash, a jagged bolt of lightning just outside our window. The whole inn shook, and the shutters rattled; even the bones in Xinot's pocket clattered, all on their own. Then a silence, green and dense in the aftermath. We waited; Hesper held the child tight in her arms.

Our darkness swirled at last, in agreement. It was a deal.

The earth settled, this time for good. The mighty clouds rolled themselves away, and the fires in the sky winked out.

In the city, the nightmare was only beginning; dust drifted from the piles of rubble, and injured children wailed. I went over to the bed, and Hesper let me lift the boy into my arms. He laid his head on my shoulder, drifting into a sleep. Our innkeeper said tiredly, "You cannot play with the world in this way."

"First you accuse us of not having any power," I said, with almost no waver at all. "And then when we show our teeth, you tell us we must cover them up again."

"You are right," she said. "And I was wrong."

"No," said Xinot. She was pulling herself to her feet, hobbling over next to me and Tad. "You were right before, old one. We haven't real power, none that we can use."

Hesper laughed shortly. She gestured at Tad. "What do you call this?"

"An anomaly," Xinot said. "A once-in-a-universe thing."

There were shouts now out in the street; the soldiers who had been waiting for Aglaia had picked themselves up and begun to wonder about her, how she and her baby had come through the storm.

"We must go," Xinot said to Serena and me, "and at once."

Hesper shook her head. "There will be chaos. Not like *that*." She nodded toward the window, where the sky was now warm and purple; we could hear evening birds beginning to sing. "But still, chaos of a sort, when they find that she has died, when their new prince goes missing."

We weren't listening to her. I handed the child to Serena in order to pack our things away. My sisters were donning their cloaks; I slung our bags around my shoulders, and Xinot grabbed her cane. We had to keep our side of the bargain, or the end would still come.

We were at the door when Hesper stepped in front of us. "Her soldiers will never let you go," she said. "Even if you manage to leave the inn, they will be searching for you all through the streets."

"We'll risk it," said Xinot.

"If they catch you, if you can't get the boy out of the city—"

"We will," I said.

Hesper shook her head. "You think it will be so simple. You think you can just walk away and everything will be fine."

Serena said, "No one notices us. No one noticed us the whole way here. Please, you must let us—"

"You think it will be easy to keep that boy away from life? Did you not see the fire of his new thread? Did you not hear the tales of his mother, of his father? Yet you think to keep their son shut away, to cage him as a dangerous bird. And you think it will be easy, and you think he will not hate you for it, in the end."

Xinot said in an undertone, "What else are we to do?"

Hesper was silent for a moment. There was a knocking now at the front door of the inn; they would be forcing it open next. "I wish," she said.

"What?" said Xinot.

"That you were different than you are."

They were yelling for her—for our girl. They didn't know yet. They would soon. Hesper flicked her filmy eyes toward the noise.

"Please," Serena said again.

Our innkeeper hesitated, and then she sighed. "Very well," she said. She reached behind to open the door for us. "I'll take you down through the kitchen. My lad knows all the secret ways. He'll bring you out of the city."

Xinot peered at her. "Will they blame you for it?"

Hesper shrugged. "Probably." She tugged the door open as the knocking turned into banging, and then crashing. She looked over her shoulder at us, as she had the first time we had met her, with that small smile, that dry voice. "But what else am I to do?"

She led us through the doorway, and my sisters slipped after her.

I paused, the last across the threshold. I turned back toward Aglaia; she lay so still, her face so calm. I hesitated, then ran quickly to her side. She smiled sweetly, as she had used to do out on our island. I passed my hand across her face, once, twice.

Of course she did not open her eyes.

So I just stood and looked at her this one last time, my friend. I wanted to remember every detail of her face. I wanted to remember how she had laughed and how her eyes had flashed and the way her voice had sounded, saying my name.

This was not her anymore; I knew that. But as long as I did not leave her, I could pretend that there was still hope. I could pretend that she would sit up and smile truly, remembering what I had done.

She had died for him, and he was alive. He was still alive.

I laid my hand on her beautiful hair, and I made her a promise.

Then somehow I managed to pull together enough of my shattered, breaking pieces to turn and leave her there alone. I didn't look back again as I followed my sisters from the room.

Hesper's kitchen lad looked at us askance when she told him to take us from the city, but he didn't argue with her. I don't suppose you would argue much with Hesper, if you were her kitchen lad. At least if the soldiers asked him if he'd seen an infant boy kidnapped, he would be able to say no, and truthfully.

He led us out the back door of the inn and through a maze of alleyways. Even in the darkest corners of this city, people were gathering, pointing up into the sky and telling one another what they had seen. Midwives were going around with bandages, and strong men were sifting through the rubble. They took no notice of us; compared to what had just happened, we were nothing to stare at.

When we reached the eastern wall, just after twilight, the lad showed us the entrance to a clever tunnel, hidden behind a broken wagon. "It's a short walk," he said, shifting a large wheel out of the way. "Just under the city wall. When you reach the end, there's a small wooden door, about the height of the boy. Wait before you open it; listen for voices, footsteps, those sorts of things. There aren't any usually, not after the sun has set. Once you're through, close the door tight and get the city behind you as quickly as you can."

Thank you, we said.

The boy blinked, then nodded warily. He gestured to Serena. "You first, with the child."

On her way past the lad, she stopped and said, "If we've a chance, we will repay you."

He swallowed. "There's no need."

We went into the dark, the four of us, and out the small door at the other end, and soon we had left Endymion's city far behind us.

We did not stop that night. We went south and east along the road we had taken as we'd followed Aglaia. Serena held Tad tight. Xinot fled with her awkward step, forcing herself fast and faster. I carried our threads, our basket, and my spindle.

As we hurried, I thought of the people we were leaving behind, not only of Hesper and the boy who had helped us, but also of the thousand hopes that would fracture because of this night. What would they do without their heroes to guide them? Endymion was dead; Aglaia was dead; their new prince, their Taddeo, was taken by the sisters of darkness, and they would never see him again.

It was a harsh fate, for a people to be leaderless. They might be torn apart by armies that Endymion's strength had kept away. They might starve without a just hand to distribute bread and dates.

We ran from them; we did not look back. But I wondered, and I hoped their threads were kinder than I feared.

Very late that night, or early the next morning, we reached the crossroads to Aglaia's old village, and the oracle was waiting. We saw her eyes first, glittering in the dark. There was no moon that night; we would not have seen it if there had been, so many clouds had gathered as the sun fell.

We stopped several feet before the woman; she stood in the center of the road, and she held her arms straight at her sides, her head tall.

Serena had just passed me the child to rest her arms, and I shifted the lad more securely in my hold, stepping out in front of my sisters.

"Let us pass," I said.

The oracle wore the same dress she had when I'd visited her—it swept, long and black, merging with the night as it had with her cave's dusk. She seemed a certain thing, a thing that would not move for horse or thunder. I shuddered, seeing her. She looked as I would have, standing out on our rocks. She loved what I had loved, and I shuddered because it thrilled me still to see her with the darkness billowing around her. It thrilled, and it twisted, sharp.

She said, low, as if she could read my mind, "Mistress, what have you done?"

I turned my face from her. I said, "We did what we must."

The oracle said, "Our power is roiling with it—betrayal. Mistress, if I had known, I would not have given you that word. If I had known, I would have held you in my cave, though you could have killed me with a touch."

I gritted my teeth against it, her purity, her absolute devotion.

"Mistress," she said, "I thought that you were mine. I thought your power and the power that I serve were the same."

There was a pause. I did not look, so I did not know if she was done.

At my back, Serena murmured, "Chloe, what is it?"

Xinot said, "We must keep going. Send her away."

I said, again, and I mustered all the authority I could find; I let my voice ring dark and deep, *Let us pass.*

The oracle did not move, but she held her palms out to the sides and said, "There is room enough for all of us."

"Come on," I muttered to my sisters.

We approached the oracle, and she stood tall, watching us. There was something I did not like in her face, some clever, knowing thing. I held Tad close, and as we moved to walk around her, I turned my face away again so as not to see her anger or the darkness or that knowing thing. So I did not see her reaching for the sheath at her back; I did not see her spinning toward us, silent, or the blade flashing dull gray in the night. I only heard a slight hiss as it came free, and a thump on the road behind me, and a sharp, surprised breath.

When I looked, the oracle's arm was raised high, pointing a knife as long and crooked as our memory toward the sky. She could not move it up or down, forward or back; her wrist was clamped tight in Xinot's hand, and my eldest sister stood, firm and gnarled as an ancient tree, staring her down.

Xinot said, "You will not do that."

The oracle was gasping, trying to wring her arm free. "I must set it right," she said, in between breaths. "I must set it right, or everything will fall."

Xinot said, "We have made our deal. It has nothing to do with you."

The oracle stopped writhing to glare at my sister. "Do you think I have not felt it?"

"It has not happened yet."

"It will." There was a pleading in her voice now. "I have felt it, old one, as well as you have with your bones. The weaving will come unwound; the sun will sink into the sea."

"No," I said. I was shaking my head. She was wrong. It had been close, but she was wrong. "We stopped that."

She turned her eyes toward me, and they were black wells in the gray of her face. "You stopped nothing. The prophecy lives. Something terrible is coming, and you will be to blame." I saw her gaze shift to the boy in my arms. "You must end it before it has begun."

Serena had frozen a few feet back on the road when the oracle drew her knife. Now she came up closer to the woman and said, "If you think we will let you kill a helpless child, you are mistaken."

The oracle said, with anger, with a passion that spat and clawed, "He is only one mortal. Have you forgotten who you are? Have you forgotten your own glory, the scent of your own power, the whisper of its dark tongue against your skin? You have known it a million, a billion more years than I have. I am only a speck in your shadow, and still I would do anything to keep it safe. Still I would die for it—I would kill a thousand such boys for it."

I was shuddering again; I did not want the oracle to know

it. I did not want her to know how it felt to look into her face, to see her rage, her surety, and to think that it didn't belong to another creature, but another time. "Let's go," I said to my sisters. "There is no way to make her understand."

"No," said Serena. "There isn't." She came over to take Tad from me, and I thought she was thinking of how I hadn't understood either, not her and her children, not Xinot and her cat. As she reached for the child, I drew a breath to tell her that I understood now—the way a mortal could seem another part of me, the way their hurts could burn and their joy glow like the sun. I wanted to tell her that you mortals were as real as the world: as true as starlight, as changeable as a wave on the sea.

But I didn't get the chance. As Xinot was stepping back to make room and I was stepping forward, holding out the boy, opening my mouth to speak, the oracle gave a sudden hiss and spun once more.

She pulled a second, smaller knife from her back; she twisted, sliding it between Xinot and Serena, into the space in the center of us, where the child was. Tad made some desperate sound. Xinot shoved the oracle back, and her knife with her.

But it was too late.

The boy was darkening with blood; she'd stabbed him, somewhere in his middle. I don't think he had the power left to scream, but he held my eyes with his sea-green ones, and there was a pleading there that sent an icy horror through me, because it was the same pleading that had been in Aglaia's eyes.

Xinot had let the oracle go; she was breathless, as Serena was breathless, as I was nothing but the trembling breath of this boy. My hands were darkening now, but I couldn't move; I couldn't put him on the ground until my sisters lowered us both down to the road, and we all huddled together there, tangled.

I held him.

What else could I do?

I held him, and he pleaded with me, and there was nothing we could do.

Again, again, again, there was nothing we could do.

I held him, and his eyes closed, and he went to join the darkness.

Time stopped happening. Nothing would ever be again; nothing had ever been. Even now, describing this moment to you, I am there again, holding the boy in my arms, and I know that this is the only moment, and it is also nothing.

Fifteen

I KNEEL WITH THE BOY, WAITING FOR THE WORLD
to end. It doesn't. I try to rage, to feel that fury building, to
give myself over to it. But there is nothing but a numbness,
an emptiness, a *why, why, why?*

I have spent my anger. There is nothing left.

Beside me, my sisters are keening; I hear them, high and
sharp. I know Serena's pain, as heavy as an ocean, as deadly
as a blade. She would have stepped in the way of that knife,
even as a mortal; she would have taken the death from this
child if she could.

Xinot's cry is more purposeful. She has anger left; she has
power lashing inside, wanting a target, wanting someone to
kill. I see her shaking with it; I hear her cane rattling as she
braces it against the rocky ground. The oracle has stepped

away from us. She is sliding down the road, watching over her shoulder, holding the bloody knife out from her side. Maybe she did not realize how we would react to this. Maybe she is surprised to see us gathered as we are around the child, bent and crying—a mourning circle, a powerless-looking thing.

Oh, it is not that we do not have power. It is that we do not use it, and do not use it. It is that we guard the world, again and again, despite the terrible cost.

Xinot pulls herself to her feet, straight as she ever gets. She glances down the road at the oracle, and for a moment I think she is going to run after her, spend her energy punishing the mortal. But she glances away again, as though the oracle isn't anything at all. The oracle saw the look too, and she scurries away now, faster than her wary sliding. She'll obey the commands of our darkness, but she'd rather not pay the price that comes from her devotion.

What does she matter anyway? Nothing now, not now the boy is dead.

I lean over him, covering him with my hair. If I hide him behind its sheen, maybe he will still exist; maybe when I pull away, he will open his sea-green eyes.

Chloe, Xinot says.

I ignore her.

Chloe, listen to me.

I shake my head.

She says, bending down right next to my ear, *Yes. You must. It is time to do our work.*

I shake my head again, hardly understanding. What does

she mean, it is time to do our work? We cannot. We cannot even think of such a thing.

But she pulls me up by the arm, and I am surprised enough not to resist. She turns me around; she opens my pack. Even here, facing away from it, I can see the glimmer of my wool at the edges of my eyes.

Oh, and I don't know how it can, but it thrills me, still. Even now, even as I hate it with the numb, dead pain that has taken me over, from the top of my head to the soles of my feet. Still something in me jumps to see it glimmering like that.

Xinot pulls out the basket of wool and my spindle; she hands them around to me. I take them, stunned at the glory, stunned at the way the glory still exists next to Tad, who seeps such horrible black in the starless night. I lower myself back to the ground, beside the boy.

I am not thinking anymore. I haven't thought since the oracle spun round with her blade, since time stopped moving in expected patterns, since I stopped being able to feel.

Serena crouches next to me, crying. That is all she is anymore—a flood of tears, as I am only a numbness. They wash her face, again and again, as the black washes Hesper's lad's tunic. My hands move of their own accord, toward the wool, toward my spindle. I listen for the next thread; it calls to me. It does not sound right, though; it sounds like pain and numbness, *why, why, why?* I don't pull that thread. I wait. I listen.

It is a strange thing that I do not hear our darkness. The darkness does not seem to exist in this numb place. Maybe if

I started to think again, it would be there, screaming at us to stop, to pay attention to what we are doing.

I listen for the thing that I want.

It is far beneath, and it is a long time before I hear it. When I do, I reach down into the basket, searching through. It is not there, and I reach deeper, past the bottom, into a space that nobody knew was there—not even me, who works with the thread every day, who knows more about this wool than anyone. I reach deeper, past the bottom, and my hand slides down and down. I am going to fall in after that, and I reach my other arm back to grab Serena's hand.

She holds it tight; I know her thoughts—she has none, just like me.

I reach; I reach. All around, the wool gleams. I dip my shoulder in, and then my head, following the faint sound of the thing I want. I do not close my eyes; I've no wish to, not when our glory swirls like this. I catch my breath at the dry burning of it.

Then Serena takes Xinot's hand, to hold herself back as she holds me back. And my eldest sister isn't numb. She isn't thoughtless. She's angry, but it's more than that. She has moved beyond anger into a knowing, certain choice, and I wonder at the surety she has. I didn't know that Xinot thought such things. I didn't know until this instant that she has been willing, all these ages long, to tear apart the universe if she was given reason enough.

She has never been afraid of that, of everything ending, and listening to her thoughts, I'm not afraid either. The wool I want is calling out to me, deeper than I knew the world could go.

I come out of the basket and look over at my sisters.

Serena's tears are flowing. Xinot is shaking with the choice she has made—not out of fear, and not only out of anger—but also out of joy at the trueness of it, the way it is the only choice we have left to make, and the way that we are the only creatures in the world who can make such a choice.

They want what I want. They will do anything to get it.

We grip hands; we will not let go. I don't look at the bleeding boy. He slid from the edge many minutes ago, and there is nothing real left of him to see.

I grab my spindle with my free hand and plunge it into the basket. My shoulder follows, then my head. It is so deep, the thing that I want, and I know what I must do. I listen; I follow. I leave the ground behind and dive in after it, and my sisters come too, linked to me, kicking through our glory.

The world disappears.

We know this stuff, this glittering mass of magic. It isn't the web of our darkness. It isn't the patterns that must never be broken, the unchangeable spun threads.

This is what the patterns are made of. This is the substance from which everything else is formed, the answers to all the questions.

Everything is here. Everything that has happened, everything that is happening, and everything that will or could or might happen in the future.

And not only that, but also things that never did happen, and that never could.

Aglaia is here, an old, old woman, saddened with many lonely years.

Tad is here, a healthy little boy, younger than he is now. He kicks a ball through the streets of his father's city, and he laughs, his hair glowing in the sun.

You are here, being born and living and dying in a thousand different ways, with a thousand different fortunes.

Everything has happened here, and everything will happen.

We forget what we came for. We drift, holding hands, and we are all weeping now at the beauty of it.

I say, *Let us never leave this place.*

My sisters do not answer, but I know that they agree.

We drift, we listen to the stories of the wool. Everything exists, all at once, and nothing ever ends.

It is a long time before we realize what is strange about this place.

We have been listening to so many lives, so much potential. Here, you mortals are unlimited, choosing one path and then the next, loving or killing or creating art so true it sends bright shivers down the back of anyone who sees it.

Everyone is here, every one of you who ever has or ever could exist.

There are no gods, though. No sun, no sea, no wisdom. There is no darkness. And there is no us.

We are nowhere in this place, not being born on our darkest night, not growing our vines on the mainland or watching the waves out on our lonely rock. We do not love or kill or create. We are nothing.

It is a long time before we notice this, but when we do, I feel a thought trickling into my head, the first of my own thoughts since the oracle spun with her second blade toward the child. My sisters feel it too. It ricochets around and through our minds, until I am speaking it: *Something's not quite right.*

I don't know what that means; of course everything is right. Everything exists. Everything goes on and on, even after it ends, even after it is gone.

But that thought is itching at me, and it doesn't go away, doesn't change, doesn't become false or unimportant.

Something is not quite right.

As I think it, we drift so far into the wool that I am not entirely sure anymore which is the way out. *It doesn't matter,* I try to tell myself and my sisters. *There is no need to leave. Everything is here.*

Still that thought itches. It itches so much that I remember what we came for, and I scan the wool again, listening for the bit we're searching out. We're so deep we've reached it; I can hear it just off to one side. We dive over to it, and I grab the bit, wind it around my spindle.

Xinot has brought her shears; I see them poking out from her free hand. Serena lets go of me and Xinot; we float there in the wool, ready to work.

I know now what I was listening for.

It isn't a mortal; it's made of the same stuff, but it has none of the bits that make up a middle or an end. It's only a beginning—a very first thought, a new breath of air, an instant that starts everything over again.

I am spinning; I am humming. My sisters watch me, knowing my thoughts.

This isn't anything that our world could bear. When we take it out into the light, it will end everything, tear apart the patterns, untangle the web. Once all has gone, this thread will be the start of a new time and a new world. And then we can spin and measure it—all the mortals, every life—exactly as we want. We can form the perfect universe, all comfort and joy. We can decide that no one will die, that lands will expand to make room for the threads that we will pile up on our endless shelves.

Existence—it will be exactly what we want it to be, with nothing bad and nothing hard and no more terrible questions. No more *why, why, why?*

I've spun the thread; it is the most beautiful thing I have ever seen.

I pass the end to Serena. Her humming has not the hint of a false note; her hands are smooth as silence as they measure the thread.

Xinot takes the place she's marked. Her shears open wide—I think the wool all around makes room, cowering away from the deadly things. The blades straddle the thread. It lies softly in my sister's hand.

I am holding my breath. Serena is staring at the thread, eyes shining brighter even than this place.

My eldest sister brings her blades together—*snap*.

Except there is no *snap*.

The moment her shears have closed and the thread has been *sliced*, it melds back together again, and Xinot is as she was before, her scissors straddling the thread, poised to cut.

She glances at us, and for the first time since Tad died, there is a hint of uncertainty in her face. Then she turns back to the thread, and she *snaps* her blades together again, and again the thread is cut.

And then it melds together, and the scissors spring apart.

I don't know how many times Xinot tries to cut the thread. Too many to count. I forget there is anything but Xinot trying, anything but sharp black shears and glittering wool, anything but this moment.

It happens so many times; if we were human, I think we would maybe have died before Xinot has finally stopped and we are drifting motionless through the wool, staring at the uncut thread.

At last, Serena says, *Maybe if we bring it out into the light.*

It takes a moment to understand what she is saying. She means out of the basket, which is where we are. She means somewhere not surrounded by all this wool, somewhere we used to be, a long time ago.

I blink, and then blink again, struggling to remember who I was before. There was something numbing. There were questions we could not answer. *Yes,* I say finally. *Maybe our power does not work in here. None of the gods are here, after all, not even our darkness, not even us.*

That is true, Xinot says. *Maybe we cannot do anything here.*

So we take hands again, and I hold my spindle, and Xinot holds her shears and the end of our newly spun thread. We dive up, away from the deep, listening for the opening to the world.

Nothing has happened since we went away. We spent ages in the wool, forgetting who we were, trying again and again to *snap* that thread. But Tad still lies by the side of the road. I catch a glimpse of the oracle still edging away, up over a hill.

In entering the basket, we left time behind. Everything happens there, so nothing does.

Xinot is holding the thread, the one that will start the universe over again. She's marked the place to cut it, where Serena measured it out. She looks up at us, making sure that we want this, too. "If I cut it," she reminds us, "everything will end."

Serena says, soft through her tears, "And everything will begin."

"Just as we want it to," I say, my voice flat as that numbness returns. "No more pain, no more terrible questions."

Xinot looks down at the thread, at her dark fingernails exactly at the end. "No more questions," she says. "Is that what you want?"

Tad's skin is so pale, so glowing, that I think he might be made of starlight. It is a beautiful thing, the way he shines. It is terrible, too, and I say, "Yes, that's what we want. No more heartbreak."

"No more death," Serena whispers.

I say, "No more endings."

Our eldest sister nods, sharp as her blades. "Very well," she says, with a sort of darkening joy. "For little Taddeo."

"For Aglaia," I whisper, and Serena takes my hand.

We watch as Xinot's scissors straddle the thread, that one last time. We watch as they come down fast, together, *slicing* through the first thought, the new breath, the instant that will start it all over exactly as we want.

Snap.

A burning sea.
A frozen fire.
Snow of ash.
Earth of wind.
Silent screams and a shrieking silence.
There is an end to patterns. The world stops spinning. The stars go out.

The universe tears itself apart, and we are to blame.

Sixteen

FIRE.

Dark, orange, filling my lungs with heat, my blood with danger. I turn to my sisters, and they are looking back at me with the same fire in their eyes, consuming them.

We are dreaming of our threads.

Still, here, at the end of this world, our glory gleams in the dark behind our lids, coil upon coil, stretching far into our minds.

They are burning. When Xinot *snapped* that thread, they really did burst into flames out there in our house at the edge of the sea. The waves rise up and the sky falls down and all our glory burns. And still we dream of them.

It's as though as we destroyed them, they leaped from the flames into our thoughts. As if we are their safe home now, as if they trust us to take care of them, despite what we have done, despite what we have chosen.

We can hear the darkness, too, howling all around us, in a panic as its patterns rip apart. Our threads are separate from the darkness, somehow. They are not angry with us. They are not asking for anything; they only spin and swirl and gleam as they have always done.

We are all three of us in pain as the world crumples. But this, the dreaming of our threads, I think is the most difficult. Even now, none of us can look away from them, our bright glory.

They murmur of what has been, of what would have been, of what happens now as the world falls apart.

Hesper is looking out the front door of her inn as streets split into chasms. She knows this is our fault. She is begging us to stop, to make it right again.

The boy who let us out through the wall is huddled in that dark space with a dozen city folk. They are hoping they will be safe, under so much stone. Of course they are wrong.

Our island, with its surging waves and rushing sky and beautiful, briny wind, is collapsing, whole rows of rocks falling into the sea.

Tad is still dead, so we cannot hear his thread. We cannot listen to all the things he might have been.

We see the oracle screaming. We see the moment when she realizes that this is her fault as much as ours, that if she hadn't killed the boy, it wouldn't have happened, not yet anyway, not so soon. She falls to her knees on the side of a hill. She puts her head in her hands; she rocks, back and forth, sobbing.

We do not feel for her. There is too much crumbling, and she is only one woman.

Mountains shift and then take off like birds into the sky.

Far-off planets begin to shriek.

The void, the emptiness between the stars, shivers, knowing even it will wink out in the end.

Before it disappears, the sun whispers in my ear, just one thing, my name. He says it as though he loves me. He knows that I have done this, but he is not angry.

He warms me until there is no such thing as warmth or sun or time.

Then all is gone.

Seventeen

NOTHING.

Can you imagine that? It is not an imaginable thing. Even we cannot understand the moment between what was and the beginning of everything.

Think of the instant before you choose a thing, what you are going to eat this morning, maybe. You don't really decide what to eat; your hand moves before your thoughts, snatching up a bit of bread, or a cup of milk, or a strand of seaweed. Your hand moves, and *then* you think, *I will eat figs*, but you think that after you have already begun to reach for them.

That moment when you are reaching—without thought, without knowing—is a little like the nothingness that comes at the end of the universe.

Except that you never grab the figs, or think, or know.

It's before the beginning. It's after the end.

There isn't anything here in the nothingness, not even waiting, not even expectation.

Not even questions.

Eighteen

THEN OUR THREAD, THE FIRST OF OUR PERFECT new universe, begins.

It is only a thought, only a breath of air.

My sisters and I breathe it in, and we open our eyes, and we look around.

I don't know how we can see, as there is no light yet. But then again, there is no dark, and we can see perfectly, in every direction.

There are so many directions. We're standing on an empty, colorless field, without any dirt or grass. It stretches limitless, without even a horizon. No one is here except for us. Nothing is here except for our clothes and Xinot's shears and my spindle and the basket of new, shining wool.

We are placed around the basket, balanced on three sides,

as though we are meant to sit around it, as though that is our purpose.

It *is* our purpose. This was the thought; this was the new beginning. Us, and the thread, and whatever world we choose, with whatever rules we think fair.

So we sit, and Xinot pulls out her shears, and I hold my spindle at the ready.

I smile about at my sisters. This is what we were made for. This moment, when we can set everything to rights.

"Who should we bring back first?" I say, because that is what we want, to bring you back. We want Aglaia and Tad and Hesper. We want everyone just the way you were. We'll only make you better, so that it does not hurt anymore, so that no child will ever be given a prophecy of pain.

Xinot has the answer. "We should bring back Monster."

Serena reaches over to touch her hand. "Oh, yes. That is what we should do."

I listen for our cat's thread. I hold my hand over the basket, and I wait until my fingers are tingling. There is no need to dive down for this thread. The basket will give us what we need; we determine the future.

There—that is the cat; I recognize his glitter.

Xinot says, "Make sure he doesn't die, Chloe."

Serena says, "Take away the pain he felt at the end."

I nod, and I only just keep from rolling my eyes at them. Of course I will. That's the point of this.

I pull out the thread and wrap it around my spindle. I think about humming some dreadful tune, but I don't know anything that fits with the perfect world we are going to make. We will have to come up with some new, better tunes. We will have to come up with new everything—new stories, new languages.

The newness of it shivers through me, and I think that it is joy.

Around and around my spindle goes. It is a perfect spindle, but then it always was. The thread glitters, and I don't let anything bad creep in. I listen for the painful parts; I tug those strands away.

Around and around my spindle goes, and the thread I hand to Serena isn't as thick as my threads usually are, but that must be how it will work here. They don't need to be thick; they're perfect as they are.

My sister takes the thread and measures it, quick and sure. She pauses, looking at the place she's marked. It's only a finger-length, this tiny thread. She frowns at me, but I remind her, "No death, Serena. The length doesn't matter when he'll live on and on."

So she passes the thread to Xinot, and our sister opens her shears.

Except they aren't shears anymore. I don't know what they are. We don't have a word for them yet; we'll have to make that up as well. They are sharp, but they are also blunt. They are long and straight, but also short and curved. They straddle the place Serena has marked, and some edge of them brings the beginning of the thread around, to lie next to the spot they are to cut. Xinot holds them wide, and then she brings them together, and the sound *rings* like a far-off bell. When she pulls her not-shears away, Monster's thread has no beginning or end; it's a circle, going around and around forever, on and on.

We stare at it.

Mew, something says.

We look down, and there he is, a kitten with soft, clean fur. He is winding around and around the basket, looking from one of us to the other to the other.

He looks up at Xinot as he passes her, and my sister reaches out a hand for him. He lets her draw him into her lap. She scratches him between the ears, just as she always used to do, and he closes his eyes, wrinkling his nose in contentment.

He is so perfect. He is so lovely and healthy and alive.

We sit there for a long time; it does not matter how long, because time doesn't really mean anything here, and Monster won't ever die.

At last Serena says, "Who else should we bring back?"

I blink and look away, remembering sea-blue eyes, sun-bright hair. "Aglaia," I whisper, and my sisters nod.

I turn to the wool again, holding that memory in my mind. I listen for the beginning of our girl's thread; there it is, waiting for me, just as it should be. I tug a strand out and wrap it around my spindle. I don't need my sisters to tell me which parts to leave out. No raiding of her village, no baby's sickness, no *pain*.

There are so few strands left when I've weeded out the imperfect ones that it takes all my skill to form an unbroken thread. It is very thin, and I hand the end carefully to Serena, afraid that it will scatter to dust.

She measures it with the lightest touch; she passes it along to Xinot.

The not-shears *ring*, and a delicate circle floats to the ground to rest alongside Monster's.

We look up, and my friend is there.

She is smiling around at us. There are no shadows on her face. There are no lines of worry or grief. She is as smooth as a polished stone, as smooth as the stones she used to gather from our shore.

That thought troubles me, and I let it drift away.

Then I stand and take the few steps toward Aglaia quickly, reaching out for her hands. She gives them to me gladly, smiling all the while. "Hello," she says. "What is your name?"

"I am Chloe," I say. I can hardly breathe, she is so real. "And these are my sisters."

"Hello," Aglaia says to them. She doesn't seem confused at how we can be sisters, with such differing ages. She doesn't seem confused by the colorless ground, either, or the way the space goes on and on.

I spin toward my sisters, eagerly. "Should we give her back her son?"

"Oh, yes," Serena breathes, and Xinot nods as well.

So I let Aglaia's hands go, but only to listen for her child's thread, the one we first formed a week ago—if weeks mean anything now, which they don't. I pull the strands, sparkling as bright as they did then. I rub off all the wrong parts—the sickness, the fear, and especially the much too early death. Serena measures the tiny thing, really only a wisp of a thread. Xinot *rings* it and it falls, big enough to fit around a very small pinkie.

For a moment I think that nothing has happened, because I am listening for something, and it is not there.

Then I realize that I was expecting a baby's cry, and of course there will be none, not in our perfect world, not where nothing hurts.

Serena reaches around the basket, to the side I cannot see. She scoops Taddeo up into her arms. He is the age he was when we first met him—all of them are, I realize, the kitten Monster and the girl Aglaia and the week-old baby Tad. Serena rocks the boy, and he sleeps peacefully. He does not murmur; he does not kick or cry. I lean over to look into his face, and I wish that he would open his eyes.

"Here," Serena says, passing him to me. She gestures toward Aglaia, and I go over to the girl.

She has taken a seat next to the basket, leaning against it as she nods off to sleep. She is not easy to wake, but when I have shaken her shoulder quite roughly, she does lift her head and smile at me.

There is no blurriness in her gaze; it is as though she went from deepest sleep to clearest wakefulness—or as though when she slept, she ceased to exist, as though she does not remember now that she did sleep.

"Hello," she says. "You are Chloe."

"Yes," I say, grinning at her.

"And these are your sisters," Aglaia says, nodding politely to them.

My grin falters. "Yes," I say. Smoothest stones gathered from our shore, that she rubs and rubs, turning in her hands.

I shake my head, to clear it. I offer our girl her baby, and she lifts her arms for him obligingly. I tell her, slowly, so she'll understand, "This is your son. This is Taddeo."

She nestles the baby close; she rubs her face against his. Watching the way he fits snug in her arms, I let out a breath, and I feel my nibbling thoughts backing away. It is going to be all right. It is going to be perfect. Aglaia has her child; all is well.

She says, smiling, "He is soft." Then she lifts her arms, offering him back to me.

I shake my head. "He's yours," I say gently, reassuring her. "He is your son."

"Oh," Aglaia says. "Thank you, Chloe. He is very soft." She holds him close again, and she strokes his hair, smiling into one of the distances.

I leave them there, as they should be, and I go over to sit in my place again between my sisters. We see Aglaia smiling; we see the baby's breath going in and out. We watch them live.

We will watch for as long as we want. When they have lived forever, we will bring back another bit of the world, and then another, and we will watch them, too. After many eternities, we will have it all just as it was, but better, truer. It is going to be all right. It is going to be perfect.

∽

Monster sleeps on Xinot's lap. Tad sleeps in Aglaia's arms. Soon Aglaia nods off as well, her cheek against the baby's forehead.

We watch them sleep, and we know that they are alive.

We watch so long that the last of the tears on Serena's face dry off, and she sits in silence with a small smile.

We watch so long that the anger I can sense coming off Xinot, as salt comes off waves on a breeze, eases, and then dissipates, into the windless space of our new world.

We watch so long that finally the numbness I have been feeling since Tad slid away starts to prickle here and there, as ice begins to sprout trickles of water underneath the sun.

As the numbness melts, I begin to know something, some wanting thing in the deep of me. It twists, and it gasps for air. There is nothing to distract me from it. Monster sleeps; Tad sleeps; Aglaia sleeps, face against her son.

I wait, and I watch the mortals sleeping. The wanting grows, as an island does. First the smallest pieces of sand, then rocks, then shipwrecked planks, boulders fallen from cliffs, and great whalebones. Up it piles, toward the sky. I wait, knowing it will break the surface in the end.

After a long time, longer even than we had lived in the other world, I turn to Xinot, and I say, "He used to purr when you did that."

Xinot glances at me. She stops scratching Monster's ears. He twitches them, once, looking up at her, and then puts his head back into his paws.

Serena says, slowly, "He used to nudge your hand when you stopped doing that."

Xinot glances at her, longer this time, and then she places Monster onto the colorless ground. He pads over next to Aglaia and curls up there instead, a tiny fuzzy ball.

Xinot says, "He used to yowl at me when I put him on the floor."

We are staring at the cat. He is alive, but instead of joy, we are feeling a strange dread, like the dread that our darkness used to pour through us, except the darkness isn't here, because we tore apart its web.

Monster sleeps; I don't know if he will ever wake again. He doesn't need to, does he? He won't starve to death. He won't feel the pain of hunger, even.

Xinot says to us, "We'll spin it again. We'll cut the thread and let it fizzle out, and we'll spin him again, the right way."

"With death, you mean?" Serena says. "With pain?"

"No. Not with death. Not with pain. Just with all the things that make Monster who he is."

I say, "We might not be able to spin it again, once the thread has gone. We don't know the rules here."

"Nonsense," Xinot says. "We're the ones who make the rules."

So I shrug. "All right. Go ahead. I'll pull the next thread when this one's gone."

Xinot takes out her not-shears again. She holds Monster's thread in one hand, and she straddles the not-shears across one edge of the circle, steady, and we're all as still as that nothingness moment between the universes.

She brings the not-shears together, and they *ring*, and when we have shaken the sound away, we look at Monster's thread.

Nothing has happened. Xinot has not cut it through; it shines as unbroken as before.

She tries again; the not-shears *ring*; Monster sleeps on next to our wool.

Xinot lowers the thread. She returns her tool to her left-hand pocket. She watches the sleeping mortals.

"Do you think they dream?" she says.

I watch them, and I want to say that they do, I want to believe it. But if it weren't for the rising and falling of Monster's tiny chest, the in and out of Aglaia's and Tad's breaths, stirring each other's hair, I wouldn't even be able to say that they were alive. Monster's nose does not twitch; his claws do not tense against the floor as they used to do when he dreamed of chasing some furry thing across our rocks. Tad's legs do not kick, and there are no dark things quivering across Aglaia's eyelids, no moments when her face tenses or she begins to weep or she remembers something she had forgotten.

"No," I say, very quietly. "I don't think they do dream."

I have never envied you mortals your dreams. Such impossible things, filled with unsatisfied longings and inescapable terrors. So I don't know why the thought of Monster and Aglaia and Tad not dreaming makes me tremble, or why when I look at Serena, she looks back with horror in her eyes.

My kindest sister says, "What have we done?"

"We've started a perfect world," I say. "What do you mean, what have we done?" But I can hear the bravado in my voice. I can hear the forcedness of it. And the deep thing growing in me gasps again, and for a moment it hurts to breathe.

Then, through the pain, an idea comes to me. I don't wait to ask my sisters what they think; I take Monster's ring of thread from where Xinot placed it on the colorless ground. I shove it into the basket of wool, as far as my arm will go. I can feel it beginning to dissolve, its fibers drifting back into the mass, its coil untwisting itself.

By the time I've pulled my arm out again, Monster has gone, disappeared, as though he never was.

I suppose that's the truth of this world now: Monster never was.

"Quick, spin it again," Serena says, and she is excited now at the prospect of what we might do.

"Make him what he was," Xinot says.

"But without the pain or the death," says Serena.

"Yes, I know," I say. "Be quiet. Let me try again."

I hold a hand out over the wool, and even though I only just shoved Monster's thread down into the basket, I can feel the bits that make his life prickling at the top of the heap again.

I smile, and I shake back my hair. If only we had known it could be this easy. If only we had understood sooner . . . but time doesn't mean anything, not here. We can try as often as we like. Whatever we don't want can go back into the basket, and we have eternity to spin the perfect threads. I show my teeth, grinning at the possibilities.

I spin Monster's thread again, and this time I listen carefully, tugging out the bits of pain and death, tucking in the bits that make him Monster—his love of Xinot, his courage jumping across our rocks, the way he hides behind the trellis of our grapes, tail lashing as he looks for birds.

It is hard, though. I tug out death and sickness, and courage comes with them. I tug out pain and uncertainty, and a great swath of Monster's love rips away, along with the eager way he watches the sky. And when I put the courage and love back in, I cannot help but add some sickness and uncertainty, too. I don't mean to. I tear the fibers into smaller and smaller pieces. But I cannot get them so small that there isn't always something I want intertwined with everything I don't.

When I hand the newly spun thread to Serena, it is hardly wider than the first. And when Xinot *rings* her not-shears closed, the circle it forms is just as small, and the Monster that appears hardly raises his head when Xinot calls his name.

He is clean and lovely. He winds around the basket, over Aglaia's legs, and he mews a clear, contented *mew*. He is alive.

You would think it would be enough, that Monster is alive.

Without saying anything, Xinot tosses me the circle again, and I throw it back into the basket. I draw out a new thread; I wind it around my spindle, and I tear out the imperfect bits. Oh, I try so hard. I wish there was a song to sing; I wish we had come up with a perfect tune. There is only silence as the spindle falls and twists, falls and twists.

I hand the thread to Serena, but I already know that it is the same as before. Xinot *rings* the thread, and we watch the cat appear, licking his already spotless paw.

Xinot says, low and harsh, "It is not Monster."

"It is," I say. "It must be. I could feel his life in the wool."

But Xinot is shaking her head. "He's missing the parts we remember. He's not the same as he used to be."

I say, "I couldn't separate them. The important parts from the problems. They were so close, I couldn't take them apart— as though they were two sides of each other, as though they were day and night."

"The sun and the moon," Serena murmurs, in a lost sort of way. "The stars and the bright blue sky."

We watch the cat and the humans sleeping for what must be another eternity.

Then the deep thing surfaces, and I know what it wants.

Heavy with how much it has grown, heavy with the hurt of each breath, I stand, and I go over to Aglaia. I shake her shoulder, very hard, knowing nothing less will wake her now. She raises her head, and she blinks at me.

"You are Chloe," she says.

"Yes," I whisper.

"And these are your sisters," she says, smiling at them.

I wait until she looks back at me. She is pretty—her eyes are blue and her hair is gold and her skin is smooth. I cannot say that she is beautiful, though, not in the way that I remember Aglaia being beautiful. And her eyes are clear, but not in a knowing way. In the way shallow water is clear, as though you can see right through.

Such smooth stones, without a bump or blemish, as empty as the face of this girl, under Serena's spell.

I say to her, "Aglaia, will you hand me Taddeo, please?"

She smiles at me. She holds out her son, and I take him into my arms. Then I bend down, carefully, and I scoop Monster up in one hand and hand him to Aglaia.

She takes the cat, nestling him against her chest just as Tad used to be. She cuddles him close, stroking his fur. She says, in her sweet voice, "Chloe, this is very soft too. Is it another son?"

I had a friend once.

Her eyes were deep as a summer sea.

Her hair was bright as the midday sun.

She smiled, and you thought the world was beautiful.

She was brave, and she was clever, and she loved her son so much that she died for him.

I watch Aglaia stroking our cat, and she doesn't know the difference between him and the child in my arms. When I look at my sisters, they are not crying or angry or as numb as I was. They know the deep thing too, and it is hurting them.

The universe stretches on and on, colorless. I hold Tad tight, looking down at him. He sleeps; he does not dream. I rock him, though I know that he cannot feel it. I tell the deep thing, again and again, that he is alive.

And Aglaia is alive, and Monster is alive. I want that to be all that I know. I want that to be all that I want. It is what I promised her, before we left her in that inn—to keep her son safe, no matter what, to the world's end.

But when Serena reaches over and grabs the circles from Xinot's feet, when she pushes them into the basket, deeper and deeper until they are nothing but wisps of wool, and the boy in my arms and the girl on the ground and our cat all wink off, and never were, I don't try to stop it. I let it happen.

And then Xinot reaches into her pocket, not the left-hand one where she keeps her shears or her not-shears, but the other one, where she kept the baby Tad's thread, and nothing else that I have seen. She draws out the thread we spun in the basket, that gave us this new beginning. It shines golden, but when I squint, I can see right through it, as I can see through our colorless ground, as I could see through Aglaia's eyes.

My eldest sister stands. She takes one of Serena's hands, and I take the other. Together we face the basket; together we circle it. Xinot shoves the thread down into the wool, and it begins to fizzle away into nothing at once.

There is just enough time for Xinot to let go of the thread, to take her hand out of the basket and grip mine, before everything goes away: limitless directions, first breath, thought.

And then we were back with the oracle at the crossroads, and it was a very dark night.

Nineteen

WHEN I HAD SHOVED MONSTER'S THREAD BACK into the basket, he had winked off, as though he never was. That had been the truth of it, when those bits of wool were where they had begun.

And the truth of this world now, after we had given back that beginning thought, was that there had never been any crumbling. No mountains had flown; no great void had shivered as it winked out.

The night was still dark. The oracle still edged away from us, down the road. We still stood beside our basket, hands empty, looking down at him. The boy. Still dead, and nothing to be done.

We didn't need to speak. I closed my packs and hefted them onto my shoulders. Xinot rubbed the head of her cane, over and again. Serena bent down to lift the boy, and he drooped in her arms like . . . I cannot describe it.

It was possible that Endymion's soldiers would be searching along this road. If we waited for them, if we told them that this was their prince, that they should burn him alongside his mother—

They would not believe us. Tad was no infant now.

If we told them who we were, if we explained everything and showed them some small magic to prove its truth—

That wasn't our way. Secrecy, hiding, not becoming involved. We knew now just how important it was; we knew now just how dangerous you mortals could be. We could not wait for the soldiers. We could not hand Tad over to some farmer or merchant along the road.

He was ours, and we would send him into the dark in the proper way—in the way they had sent his father, in the way they would send his mother.

We left the road; we left the oracle still watching us warily.

We walked together over the hills, over ground that was so colorful, even on this night. It was black, yes, but also blue and purple and silver and deepest green. It shimmered with all the colors that there were. I didn't know what we would find at the top of each rise; I didn't know how the slope would bend, and I felt the rightness of that, the not knowing.

A few hills away from the road, we stopped and stood in our half circle, watching the clouds, watching the colorful hills. The shadows danced beneath my sisters' eyes. Their skin glowed as the boy's did, bloodless in Serena's arms.

It was an easy thing, to call the fire up. It was as easy as calling our cooking fire in our island house. The flames spat and swam, eager, alive. They would not jump the pit we had given them, but they wanted to. They wanted to eat the world up. They wanted to gobble the sky.

It was hard to give the boy to them. I don't know if Serena ever could have. She was holding him so tightly, and her cheek was on his hair. I went over next to her; I touched her arm.

"We must let him go," I said, trying to convince myself that it was a possible thing to do.

She looked up at me; there was wildness in her gaze. I blinked, and I remembered another pair of flashing eyes; as my sister spoke, I remembered another beautiful, terrible question, in another harsh voice. "How can you, Chloe?" Serena said. "How can you let him be dead? How can you give him up? He's only a little boy."

I didn't know. Not how I would stand when it was done or continue down the road. I didn't know how I would breathe after this, but I knew that I would. The boy had died, as his mother had died, and we would go on and on.

I said, "There's nothing else to do, Serena. Do you want to go back to that colorless place?"

My sister looked away. She said, so low, "You don't understand. You've never understood. You've never loved them like we have."

"Serena," Xinot said, behind us, "you don't mean what you say."

"She never has! Not Monster, not any of them. She's never

cared for anything but her own comfortable existence."

"Is our existence comfortable?" Xinot said. "I didn't know."

Serena was rocking and rocking now, bending over the boy. "You know what I mean. You said it too. She's too young to understand things. She's too young to love like we do."

I told them, "I loved Monster."

Serena shook her head.

"I did. Xinot said something once, about me spinning that thread, the one that would have ended it all then. I thought she was wrong, but now I know that she was right. I was angry after I stopped her from cutting it because a part of me had wanted her to. I couldn't admit that; it terrified me.

"And I loved Aglaia, before either of you did. I couldn't admit that, either—did that make me young? But I know now that I loved her, so maybe I am less young than I was."

"You?" Xinot's voice floated between us, a dark spark. "You will never grow up, Chloe, and Serena will never grow old."

"And you will never be young," I said. "Yes, I know." I thought of the prayers that my girls send me, filled with passion and longing, and I knew that I was wrong, and Serena was wrong. Love doesn't leave us young ones alone.

After all, I recognized my sister's anger; I recognized it because it was mine—the need to lash out, to blame someone. I had done that so many times, not wanting to accept what was. I had done it to my sisters, and to Hesper, and even to the oracle. It was hard to accept this now—that the boy was dead, and his mother was dead, and there was nothing to be done. Oh, it would be easy to rant and rave. It would be easy to scream, to rage, to turn our backs on our calling. But we had done that, and nothing had changed.

There was a chill wind blowing; it threw my hair about, and I looked up, to where the clouds were blowing too, and the stars were coming out. How were you supposed to keep on going? It was what Aglaia had wanted to know, when the world had given her *pain*: what there was left to live for now.

My sisters and I were motionless, watching the clearing sky. There had been no clouds in that colorless place, and no wind, and no stars. So we had never once seen the dark opening like this, or felt this murmur on our skin, or heard this twinkling song.

It was just a faint hum, a small trickle like a brook along smooth rocks. The stars are so far away, we can only ever hear them on a night like this one—when there is no moon, and the clouds are gone, and the wind is dying down; when it seems the whole world is cool and still and every bird is sleeping. Then, if we listen, if we do not even breathe, we might hear their voices, a shimmering drizzle of sound.

We listened. We tried not to breathe. We had heard this song, oh so many times, out along the edge of our sea. We had known it so well as belonging to the stars that when we heard it in another voice, in another place, we hadn't recognized it.

It was a small tune, a hum of violets dripping with rain, of rich dark soil, ready for tilling. It was a song from the middle of life, where each waking and each sunset is fulfillment. One such day, this song said, might be reason enough for a life.

It was the song Aglaia had been singing when we had paused outside the door to her room. It was the song we had heard as she pushed the baby Tad into the world. Then it had been joyful, and now it was so quiet and so soft—there was a sadness in it, but I did not want it to stop. It cradled me, even as it made the tears come. It wasn't broken; it was overflowing, like Aglaia's face had been, looking at her son.

We listened. We let our hair drift in the cold air, and we felt our magic everywhere, and we listened to the stars singing our friend's song.

When they were done, I turned to my sisters, still letting the tears fall.

Xinot was hunched, twisted away; her cloak hid what was on her face.

But I could see that Serena was crying too, as she had cried before out in that hallway, when she had told me that it was always a miracle for there to be beautiful things.

I held her gaze so she could see the starlight striking patterns all down my cheeks. I reached out my arms for the child, and she kept him one moment, one moment more. Then she gave him to me, and somehow, still hearing the echo of Aglaia's song, I let him fall out of my hands and into the fire.

We watched him burn.

He was so small, and our fire was so hot. It ate his spilled blood first, and Hesper's lad's tunic, and his bright hair. It nibbled at his toes. It poured down his throat to his lungs. Bits of him wisped away, as strands of a thread. His thread would have wisped like that in Xinot's right-hand pocket, after the oracle stabbed him.

We watched until there was nothing left but fire and wisp and ash.

As we turned away at last, the sun was just beginning to rise, and he touched the edges of my tears with pale fingers, but he did not speak. He had loved the boy, with his golden hair, with his sea-green eyes. He had loved Aglaia, and he wept as well to see that her boy had died.

Yes, that morning, as the sun came up, he wept.

He still rose, though, and when our Tad was gone away into that place we cannot touch, we left him there and we went south, toward the sea again.

We left the fire burning. It would burn much longer than a fire should. A mortal might see it and fear it—and it will be good if you do. It is a fearful thing, with a terrible hunger.

It was late afternoon when we came at last to our island today. It had been so long. It had been a lifetime, and more, since we had smelled our sea, and it was sweeter than honeycomb and sharper than aged cheese.

Our rocks stretched, beautiful, out into the waves. The sandy cliffs were a faint brown line, and the surf that broke on them sent up a smidge of spray. I squinted out into the gray and blue, feeling the world sweep through me, warming me like a wondrous wine. As my sisters and I climbed from our rocky way, my friend was tossing his light, so that as the spray danced and somersaulted, it was dazzling bright.

Inside our house, Xinot called the fire pit into existence with a quick word. We looked about at our shelves of thread, untoppled, safe on our island. We could imagine ourselves surrounded by piles of coins, they looked so precious in the firelight. It was as though we had never left. It was as though the crisis had never come.

We stood in silence, blinded by them, watching the light slide along their lengths, onto our skin. When Xinot began to hum, I did not notice at first, it was so soft and melting. But then the notes must have gotten inside, edged themselves between my bones, because my fingers began to itch, as they hadn't done in weeks, and my blood began to stir.

I saw Serena's eyes light up as she heard this tune. She joined in; she stretched the melody out, and it flitted and spun; it flipped and shimmered long. While they hummed, my sisters watched me. They were waiting. They were asking if I was ready yet.

I didn't answer them. I didn't join in, either, but I went to the door where I had left my packs. I undid the strap I hadn't touched since we had left the boy's fire burning on that hill.

We have to believe in it, you know. We have to become it—the spinning and the drawing out and the *slicing*, the hidden pattern, the question that comes from the dark. When we fall fully into it, we become one another, the hands that pass the thread, connecting us to the others, beginning to middle to end.

I hadn't the single-minded devotion of that oracle, not

anymore. But I was still Chloe, the quickest, the loveliest, and when my pack fell open, there our glory shone.

My sisters pulled over our stump and chair and stool, and I let Xinot's music wrap me round. I added my voice, a quick, sharp counterpoint. I took up my spindle, and Xinot drew out her scissors. I reached down into my wool and pulled out the first strand, listening to what it wanted to be. There was pain and sadness; there was death in this wool. But I took nothing out and I added nothing in. I passed the thread to Serena, and she measured it, long and shining, and Xinot's shears were shears again. Somewhere on this world, a mortal was born, and it would not live forever.

We stopped; the knowledge that it would not live forever sliced us like a jagged rock, like a sharp blade. But as we stopped, as that mortal was born, we felt something waking beneath our tune. It was dark, and it was beautiful. We turned our faces to the newly coiled thread, and we saw it dancing there, our shadow.

Light and dark, day and night: The shine of that thread and our magic spun and shimmied, intertwined. Oh, it hurt to watch, like too much knowledge hurts, like never being able to sleep.

But that dance was sliding underneath our skin, as a haunting tune had, long ago, as the eyes of a girl had, as the scrunchy face of her son—and it did not matter if the darkness and the mortals were at odds. They were both inside of us, hard and fiery, both tearing at the place where we would keep a soul. And even though it hurt, so that we could hardly breathe, we didn't falter, and we didn't shudder—we spun, and we measured, and we *sliced* with one will, and the world whirled beautifully.

When night fell, we left our work to go out to the stars and the sea. We stood there together, conversing with our magic, listening to the prayers of the day. Xinot listened to the muttering of crones, Serena to mothers' pleas.

I watched the clouds billow and my half-moon gleam. I breathed in deep, and I closed my eyes to hear the praying of my girls. I felt our darkness churning along the wind, weaving with their words.

There had been another night, when Serena hadn't noticed that our darkness was swirling in a strangely deliberate way. Aglaia had been sleeping in the house at our backs, and I had been so sure that I could take her out and drown her the next day, and nothing would stop me.

And there had been many nights when I hadn't been able to hear our darkness at all, for the sound of Aglaia's song, catching in my mind. My sisters hadn't ever known of that; I hadn't told them, because I had still been sure—oh, so sure— that the girl held no danger for me. That I could keep us safe.

I had been wrong. Even now, I could hardly believe how wrong I turned out to be.

The world did not end, not unalterably.

But it could have. If Hesper hadn't threatened to kill the boy; if she'd let it all fall then, without that one tearing thread to bring it back . . . Or if we were different from what we are, and we hadn't loved your world enough to return . . .

I don't know what might have happened. It is a dangerous riddle, and one that must never be answered.

Oh, you mortals, with your desperate prayers, with your terrible fates. You all want something from us—you all think there must be an easier way, a shortcut through the harder parts of life.

There is no shortcut. There never is anything we can give you. You must live the life you have; it's all that any of us can do.

I know it is hard to accept this, though, and I know that sooner or later one of you will turn up on our island, demanding our help. And you mustn't, not anymore. We couldn't bear it now; we aren't the same as we once were. Oh, I am still young, and Xinot is still old, and Serena is still middle-aged. We cannot measure our lives in years, not as you do.

We can measure our hearts by how many times they have broken, though. We can measure our love by how much we have lost.

The sun is about to rise; before he opens his eyes, these winds will take the words I have been whispering all this night across your mortal world. They will find you. They will bring my story to your ears, and my prayer, which is this:

Do not seek us out. Do not come looking for adventure or knowledge. Do not come asking for a new spinning of your thread. Stay away. It is better this way.

I know the true danger now.

It is not that you make us forget our work; it is not that

we betray ourselves for you. It is that you are everything we already love. You are our glory: bright, breathtaking. You are the wool and the measure and the *snap*. The death you are weighted with makes your days precious; the pain of living makes you brave. Your questions are beautiful, your dreams are impossible because of the mystery of your fate.

Do not seek us out, mortal. Do not appear one afternoon on our doorstep, with your sea-colored eyes, with your sun-colored hair. You must understand: It is too late for me now. I could not help it if you came, no matter how hard I might try. I could not help it, and the world might fall, this time unalterably.

You must stay away. It is the only thing left to do.

It is too late for me to keep from loving you.

Acknowledgments

To my family, thanks a thousand times for support, for listening, for believing.

To my friends, thanks for enthusiasm and perspective and strength. Special thanks to Sara for pivotal encouragement and to Rob for a necessary world's ending.

And to Reka Simonsen, thanks always for watching for beauty, pointing to cracks, and fighting.

REBECCA HAHN grew up in Iowa, attended college in Minnesota, and soon afterward moved to New York City, where she worked in book publishing and wrote her first novel, *A Creature of Moonlight*, on the side. Her fate has since led her to Minneapolis. She misses the ocean but loves to watch stars shine bright. Visit her at rebeccahahnbooks.com.